Born to Run

Flip the pages to see Best Mate run!

Michael Morpurgo is one of Britain's best-loved writers for children and has won many prizes, including the Smarties Prize, the Whitbread Prize, the Red House Children's Book Award and the Blue Peter Book Award. From 2003 to 2005 he was the Children's Laureate, a role which took him all over the UK to promote literacy and reading, and in 2005 he was named the Booksellers Association Author of the Year.

Also by Michael Morpurgo:

Alone on a Wide Wide Sea *
The Amazing Story of Adolphus Tips *
Private Peaceful *
The Butterfly Lion *
Cool!
Toro! Toro!
Dear Olly *
The Dancing Bear
Billy the Kid *
Farm Boy *

* *Also available on audio*

Born to Run

michael morpurgo

Illustrated by Michael Foreman

HarperCollins *Children's Books*

This edition produced for
The Book People Ltd,
Hall Wood Avenue, Haydock, St Helens, WA11 9UL

First published in hardback in Great Britain by HarperCollins *Children's Books* 2007
HarperCollins *Children's Books* is a division of HarperCollins*Publishers* Ltd
77–85 Fulham Palace Road, Hammersmith, London W6 8JB

The HarperCollins *Children's Books* website address is
www.harpercollinschildrensbooks.co.uk

1

Text copyright © Michael Morpurgo 2007
Illustrations © Michael Foreman 2007

The author and illustrator assert the moral right to be
identified as the author and illustrator of this work

ISBN 978-0-00-787473-6

Printed and bound in Great Britain by
Clays Ltd, St Ives plc

Mixed Sources
Product group from well-managed
forests and other controlled sources
www.fsc.org Cert no. SW-COC-001806
FSC © 1996 Forest Stewardship Council

FSC is a non-profit international organisation established to promote the
responsible management of the world's forests. Products carrying the FSC
label are independently certified to assure consumers that they come
from forests that are managed to meet the social, economic and
ecological needs of present and future generations.

Find out more about HarperCollins and the environment at
www.harpercollins.co.uk/green

To Simon, Alison,
Rose, Amy, Hazel
and Otto

"Best Mate for ever"

Part of Patrick's walk to school, to St Thomas' Junior School on Porthcressa Road was along the canal, past the brown sauce factory which somehow smelled both sweet and sour at the same time. That walk along the canal where the barges chugged by, where the ducks dipped and drank, was the only part of going to school that Patrick looked forward to at all. There was so much he was dreading. He sat there on his bed and thought about the school day ahead of him, wishing he didn't have to live through it. The radio was burbling downstairs as it always was, and his dad had burnt the toast, again.

Patrick thought of Mr Butterworth, his teacher and football coach, whose literacy homework – that stupid story about someone you meet standing in a shopping queue – he still hadn't finished, and who this time was bound to make him stay in after lunch and finish it. That meant that the head teacher, Mrs Brightwell, would probably find him there, and so he'd be in double trouble. She was always on at Patrick about being untidy or running in the corridors, or day-dreaming or using what she called 'lazy words', such as 'cool' or 'wicked', or worst of all, 'whatever'.

If she ever heard anyone saying 'whatever' she'd practically explode, especially if you shrugged your shoulders at the same time. The trouble was that just at the moment and for no good reason, 'whatever' happened to be Patrick's favourite word. He knew it irritated his mum and dad as well, knew how much Mrs Brightwell hated it, but the word would just pop out as if it had a mind of its own, and with it came a shrug. There was nothing he could do to stop himself, and of course all too often Mrs Brightwell would be right there, and she'd blow up. After it was over, everyone would turn round and laugh at him. That was what Patrick dreaded most about school, being laughed at.

He dreaded Jimmy Rington too, Jimbo to his friends, and Patrick wasn't one of them, not since the day before when he'd let in *that* goal, the goal that had lost the cup final against Burbage School. It hadn't been Patrick's fault, not entirely. It was the kestrel's fault as well. The thing was, he'd been watching for the kestrel on and off for days. The bird was roosting high up on the chimney of the brown sauce factory. Patrick loved to see him come swooping down and hover there over the long grass at the edge of the playing field. Patrick could have watched him all day and every day. Once he'd caught sight of the kestrel he couldn't take his eyes off him. It wasn't his fault that he came gliding over the football pitch at just the same moment the Burbage centre forward let fly with a speculative long range shot that Patrick should easily have saved.

There was all the sudden shouting, as the ball rocketed past him into the net, and he was left diving after it despairingly, ending up flat on his face in the mud. When he looked up, there were Jimmy Rington and the others running towards him, yelling and screaming: "Loser! Loser!" Mr Butterworth said it wasn't the end of the world, but to Patrick it certainly felt like it. So Patrick had a lot of worrying to do that morning.

He was late down to breakfast as a result. He barely had time to feed Swimsy, his goldfish, and shovel down his Cocopops, before his mum was kissing him goodbye on top of his head as she passed by behind him, talking as she went, not to him at all, but to Patrick's dad, about not forgetting to get the car serviced. Then she was out of the door and gone. Minutes later Patrick was being hustled into the car, and his dad was telling him to be careful crossing the road by the school, to wait until the lollipop man said he could cross – this was what he said every morning.

Patrick was dropped off by the bridge as usual, and found himself alone at last and walking along the canal. Suddenly it didn't matter any more about Jimmy Rington or the goal he'd let in, or saying 'whatever' or Mrs Brightwell's volcanic temper tantrums. He breathed in the sweet and sour smell of the brown sauce factory. It was strange, he loved the smell, but hated the taste of the actual sauce. Shading his eyes against the sun, he looked up at the chimney to see if his kestrel was there. He wasn't, but Patrick didn't mind, because there were some ducks cruising past him, and another nearby with his bottom in the air, and that always made him smile. A moorhen scurried across the towpath in front of him and disappeared into the long grass.

He hitched up his school bag and felt suddenly all bright and breezy, until he saw the swan some distance ahead of him, standing there on the towpath, looking at him, waiting for him. That worried him, because Patrick knew this swan, knew him all too well. They had met once before. It looked like the same one who had blocked his path on the way to school only a couple of weeks ago. He'd come running at Patrick wings

outstretched, neck lowered to attack and hissing like a hundred snakes. Patrick had had to run into the undergrowth to escape him and had fallen into a patch of nettles. So Patrick did not like this swan, not one bit. Yet somehow he was going to have to get past him – it was the only way to get to school, and he had to get to school. The question was how to do it.

Patrick stood there eyeing the swan, just hoping that sooner rather than later the swan would decide it was time to go back into the water. But the swan stayed steadfastly where he was, glaring darkly at him, his great black feet planted firmly on the towpath. He was showing no signs of moving anywhere.

Patrick was still wondering what to do, when out of the corner of his eye he saw something floating out in the middle of the canal. It was bright green and looked plastic – a sack of some kind. He probably wouldn't have paid it any more attention – a sack's not that interesting, after all – if he hadn't heard the squeaking. It sounded as if it was coming from the sack itself, and that didn't make sense.

Patrick thought at first it might have been the piping of ducklings or moorhen chicks – he'd heard them often enough on the canal. But then he remembered that there weren't any chicks around, not any more, because it was autumn. The whole place was carpeted with yellow leaves, gold leaves, red leaves. They were all around his feet. Spring and summer were over. No, it really had to be the sack itself that was squeaking.

It was still early in the morning and Patrick's brain must have been working very slowly, because several moments passed before he realised that there was something alive inside the sack, and even then it wasn't only the squeaking that convinced him. The sack, he noticed, wasn't just drifting gently along like everything else, the leaves, the sticks, all the other flotsam in the canal. It was turning of its own accord, as if it was being propelled from the inside. There was definitely something inside it, and whatever it was seemed to be struggling against the side of the plastic sack, kicking at it, trying to escape from it and squeaking and squealing in terror. He had no idea what it might be, only that it was alive and in danger of drowning. The canal wasn't that wide. It was dirty but it wasn't wide. He could do it.

Patrick didn't think about it any more. He shrugged off his school bag and leaped into the canal. He knew he was a good enough swimmer, so he wasn't worried about drowning, only about getting cold and wet. He didn't want the canal water in his mouth either, so he kept it tight shut. Just a few quick strokes out into the canal and he'd grabbed the sack, turned, and

was swimming back again. Suddenly the bank seemed a long way away, but he got there.

Climbing out was the most difficult part because his clothes were heavy and clinging, and

the sack was slippery in his hands, difficult to
hold on to. He felt suddenly very weak, felt the
cold of the water chilling him to the bone. But
with one huge effort he heaved himself up,

 17

enough to hook one leg up, on to the bank, and then he was out. Standing there, dripping from everywhere, he untied the sack and opened it. There were five puppies inside, leggy, gangly looking creatures, skeletal almost, all of them trembling with cold and crawling over one another, squirming to get out, mouths open and squeaking frantically. They were like no puppies Patrick had ever seen before.

He had two choices, and he knew neither of them were any good. He could go home at once and leave the puppies in his bedroom – he had a key, he could easily let himself into the flat. There'd be no one home, but at least they'd be warm there. This way he could change his wet clothes too. He could feed them when he got back after school. The trouble was that it would take for ever to get there and back, and by the time he got to school he'd be so late that Mrs Brightwell would probably have one of her eruptions and he'd be in detention for a week, and she'd be bound to send him home with another cross letter for his mum and dad.

She certainly wouldn't believe his excuse: "Please Mrs Brightwell, sorry I'm late, but I had to jump into the canal on the way to school to rescue some puppies." If he didn't have the puppies with him, and he'd already changed into dry clothes, she'd be bound to think he was making the whole thing up. She hated excuses anyway, especially incredible ones. She'd go ballistic.

Or he could go straight to school all wet and smelly from the canal, only a little bit late and carrying the puppies with him. At least she'd have to believe his story then, wouldn't she? But then he thought of what Jimmy Rington would say when he walked into school all dripping and sodden, how everyone would laugh at him. They'd never let him forget it, that was for sure. And then there was that swan he had to get by, still there blocking his path, still glaring at him.

In the end it was Mr Boots, the lollipop man, who made up Patrick's mind for him. Patrick was standing there, numb with cold, still wondering what he should do, when he saw Mr Boots come hurrying along the towpath, lollipop stick in his hand, his white coat flying. Patrick had never much liked Mr Boots. He wasn't called "Bossy Boots" for nothing. He was a bit full of himself, a bit puffed up and pompous. And there was something about him Patrick had never quite trusted. He was a bit of a phoney, Patrick thought. But all the same he was glad to see him now.

Mr Boots arrived breathless. For a while he could only speak in gasps. "You jumped in!" he spluttered. "Whatever d'you want to go and do that for?"

By way of an answer Patrick showed him what he had in his sack. Mr Boots bent over to look. Then he was spluttering again. "Blow me down! Puppies, greyhound puppies they are. Little beauties!" He looked up at Patrick. "You could have drowned yourself, doing that. Look at you, you're soaked to the skin. You'll catch your death standing here. Best get you into school and fast. I'm telling you, when Mrs Brightwell hears about this... You come along with me. Here, you can take my lollipop stick if you like, and I'll carry your school bag and the puppies."

As the two of them hurried along the towpath a barge came chuntering past. "Been in for a bit of a dip, have you, son?" laughed the man at the wheel. But Patrick paid him no attention – he had his eye on that swan. He felt a little more confident though, because he had the lollipop stick to wave now. As it turned out he didn't need it. The swan moved aside as they came hurrying towards him and swam out into the canal, riding the wake of the barge. Then they were up the steps from the towpath and across the road into the school playground.

Patrick knew he was already late the moment he walked through the door. There was no one about. They'd all be in assembly by now. He'd be in really big trouble. He felt like running off home there and then. But he couldn't, because Mr Boots had him firmly by the hand and was walking him down the corridor towards the hall. He could hear Mrs Brightwell's voice now. She was making one of her important announcements, and by the sound of her she was in full flow and already cross about something. *Not a good moment to interrupt her*, Patrick thought. Mr Boots stopped at the door to straighten his tie and smooth down his hair – he didn't have much of it, but what he had he liked to keep immaculate. Then, clearing his throat, he threw open the double doors, and in they went.

Everyone turned and gawped. Up on the platform Mrs Brightwell stopped in mid-sentence. A deep hush fell around them as they walked the entire length of the hall up towards Mrs Brightwell. Every step Patrick took seemed to squelch louder than the one before, and all the way the puppies in the sack were squealing and squeaking.

Mrs Brightwell did not look at all pleased. "Mr Boots," she said, "what is this? Why is Patrick standing there dripping all over my assembly hall? What on earth has happened?"

"Actually, it's a bit of a long story, Mrs Brightwell." Mr Boots sounded typically self-important. "You had to see it to believe it. There I am, just minding my own business on the crossing outside the school, when I hear this splash. So I look over the bridge, and what do I see? Only young Patrick here in the canal swimming like a fish. Well of course I think he's fallen in, and he's drowning. So I start running, don't I? I mean I've got to save him, haven't I? But then I see he's not drowning at all. He's got hold of this sack and he's swimming like billy-o for the bank. And I'm thinking to myself: *You're off your tiny rocker, my son, taking a dip in that filthy old canal just to fetch out a dirty old plastic sack.* Luckily for young Patrick here I was on hand to help him out, cos he

wouldn't have made it on his own, that's for sure."

You fibber! Patrick thought. *You great big fibber!* But he didn't say anything.

Mr Boots hadn't finished yet. He was enjoying his moment in the limelight. "So Patrick's standing there now on the bank, all shivering and shaking, and that's when I have a little look inside the sack, don't I? And what do I find? It's full of puppies, that's what, five of the little beggars, and if I'm not mistaken, which I'm not, they're greyhounds, about seven weeks old by the look of them. We've got brindles in there, blacks and a fawn one too. I go down the greyhound track from time to time, so I know my greyhounds. I'm what you might call a greyhound connoisseur. They're lovely pups too, fine dogs. And young Patrick here jumped in the canal and saved them. I saw him with my own eyes. He's a bleeding hero, if you ask me – 'scuse my French, Mrs Brightwell – but that's what he is, a bleeding hero."

Patrick had never heard such a depth of silence as he heard in that hall when Bossy Boots had finished. Then one of the puppies squeaked, and suddenly they were all at it, a whole chorus of squealing, yelping puppies. "Aaah, sweet," said someone. Someone else started giggling, and soon there was laughter and clapping too, rippling round the hall. Within moments the assembly hall was loud with cheering and whooping – one or two were yelping like puppies.

Patrick stood there soaking in the applause and feeling about ten foot tall. Even Mrs Brightwell was clapping now. Patrick saw there were tears in her eyes as she beamed at him. That was the first time, Patrick thought, that she'd ever beamed at him. He'd never seen her cry before either; he didn't know she could. Suddenly he found himself really quite liking her, and that hadn't happened before either.

As the applause died away at last, Mrs Brightwell came down off the platform, and peered into the sack. "One. Two. Three. Four, five, and they're all alive because of you, Patrick. What you did was very special. You risked your life to save them. I think that's about as special as it gets." She looked into the sack again, shaking her head sadly now. "Beautiful creatures. Beautiful, but unwanted it seems. So sad, and so wicked too."

Her voice was trembling with anger as she spoke to the whole school. "It's difficult to believe, children. I won't hide from you what must have happened. Someone tried to get rid of these puppies, tried to drown them in the canal. And if Patrick here hadn't jumped in and..." For a moment she could hardly speak. "And we mustn't ever let the wicked people have their way, must we Patrick? That's why we must report this at once to the Police."

She had her hand on Patrick's shoulder now. Although he was still all aglow inside, he must have been shivering, because Mrs Brightwell suddenly noticed it. "Goodness gracious," she said. "We're standing here nattering away, and this poor boy is half frozen to death. We'll have three loud cheers for Patrick, children, and then we'll get him into a hot shower and warm him up. He'll be needing some dry clothes too – we've got plenty in the lost property cupboard. Three cheers then for Patrick and his puppies! Hip, hip!"

Patrick walked out of the assembly hall that morning on Cloud 9, the three cheers and one for luck ringing in his ears. But the best moment of all was when he caught Jimmy Rington's eye. He was looking somewhere between gutted and gobsmacked, which made Patrick feel he was up there and floating on Cloud 109.

Everything was a bit of blur after that. Patrick had the longest, hottest shower of his life in the teachers' bathroom. He shivered all the cold out of him, and washed away the slime and stench of the canal. They found some clean, dry clothes, along with a school sweatshirt that was far too big for him, and a pair of trainers that were too small for him. Mr Butterworth found a cardboard box and a blanket for the puppies, and set it down by the radiator in Mrs Brightwell's room, which was where Patrick spent the next hour or so, kneeling by the box, playing with them, watching them bask in their newfound warmth. He loved them licking his fingers and chewing on them. They had sharp little teeth, but Patrick didn't mind.

There was one that Patrick loved at once more than the others, the fawn one. To Patrick he wasn't fawn at all. He was golden, and his eyes were hazel brown and shining. But it wasn't what he looked like that mattered most to Patrick. He loved him because every time he put his hand into the box, the fawn puppy was right there looking up at him, almost talking to him with his eyes. Patrick understood at once that this was the one

who needed him most. So he talked to him, told him where he lived, about his mum and dad, about Swimsy, about how he'd always wanted a dog of his own, and now that he'd found one he was going to take him home, and they'd go up on the park where he could run as far as he wanted to, for as long as he wanted to, that he'd look after him for ever and ever. And Patrick knew the puppy was listening to every word, believing and trusting everything he said. That was when Patrick picked him up for the first time and took him on to his lap.

Patrick promised him then and there that he'd never ever let any harm come to him again, that he was his friend for life, his best mate for ever. He gave him a name too. He thought and he thought, but he just couldn't come up with a name that seemed to suit him – Lucky, Jack, Bob, Rex, Henry, nothing worked – which was why, in the end, he didn't give him a proper name at all.

Instead he called him the only name that kept coming into his head, again and again, Best Mate. Best Mate seemed pleased enough with it, and Patrick was sure the puppy was already beginning to recognise his name every time he repeated it. And the more he said it, the more Patrick knew this was just the right name for him, that it suited him perfectly, because this dog was his dog, his best friend, nobody else's.

Patrick didn't know it, because no one had told him, but they'd phoned his dad at work. In fact, as it turned out, they'd called a whole lot of people. His dad and the police, the school nurse and a reporter from a local newspaper arrived all together. Everyone said how wonderful he'd been, which Patrick liked a lot, and everyone wanted to ask him questions, which he liked less. The policewoman was full of questions: about where exactly he'd jumped in, whether he'd seen the person who'd thrown the sack into the canal, or noticed anyone running away. The school nurse felt his head and took his pulse, and asked him whether he'd swallowed any canal water. She kept on asking him how he was feeling. Lots of them asked how he was feeling. So he told them. He said he felt fine, but that he wanted to keep Best Mate and take him home after school, that he knew he didn't have room at home for all five. The others could go to the rescue centre, couldn't they? He only wanted one, he was happy with one, just so long as it was Best Mate.

Then his mum came running in all of a fluster. They'd called her at work too. So by now there was quite a gathering in Mrs Brightwell's office, and Bossy Boots was telling anyone who would listen about what had happened, about how lucky it was for Patrick that he'd been there to help him out of the canal. Patrick thought of telling everyone that actually he'd helped himself out of the canal, but he couldn't be bothered – it just didn't seem that important to him. All that really mattered now was taking Best Mate home with him and looking after him. His mum kept hugging and kissing him. Patrick wasn't so keen on that, not with everyone else there. So in the end he turned and walked away. He was tired of all the talk, all the chatter going on around him. He wanted to be alone with Best Mate.

But they wouldn't leave him alone. Within a couple of minutes he found there was someone else crouching down beside him. He had on a blue uniform and a peaked cap. He explained he was from the RSPCA. He spoke with a very soft understanding voice, the kind people use when they know you're not going to like what they're about to say – a bad news voice. He had come to take the puppies away, he told Patrick, and look after them for him. "We'll find good homes for them all, Patrick. OK?" he said.

"I've got a good home," Patrick replied. "So I

can keep one of them, can't I?" He looked up at his dad, "We can, can't we, Dad?" But his dad wasn't saying yes and he wasn't saying no. He was looking down at the floor and saying nothing. His mum was biting her lip. She wouldn't look at him either. That was the moment Patrick realised for the first time that they might not let him take Best Mate home with him.

His dad was crouching down beside him now, his arm around him. "Patrick," he said, "we've talked about this before, about having a dog, haven't we? Remember what we said? We can't keep a dog in the flat. Mum's out at work most of the day. You know she is, and so am I. It wouldn't be fair on him. That's why we got Swimsy instead, remember? You did such a brave and good thing, Patrick. Mum and me, we're so proud of you. But keeping one of these pups just isn't on. You know that. He needs space to play, room to run in."

"We've got the park, Dad," Patrick pleaded, his

eyes filling with tears now. "Please, Dad. Please."
He knew it was hopeless, but he still wouldn't
give up.

In the end it was Mrs Brightwell who persuaded
him, and that was only because he couldn't argue
with her. No one argued with Mrs Brightwell.
"Tell me something, Patrick," she said, and she
was talking to him very gently, very quietly, not
in her usual voice at all. "You didn't save those
puppies just so you could have one, did you?"

"No," he replied.

"No, of course you didn't," she went on. "You're
not like that. You saved them because they were
crying out for help. You gave them their lives
back, and that was a truly wonderful thing to do.
But now you have to let them go. They'll be well
looked after, I promise you."

Patrick ran out then, unable to stop himself
sobbing. He went to the toilet, where he always
went when he needed to cry in private. When he

got back, the box and the puppies had gone, and so had the man in the peaked cap from the RSPCA.

Mrs Brightwell told Patrick he could have the rest of the day off school, so that was something. His mum and dad took him home in the car. No one spoke a word all the way. He tried to hate them, but he couldn't. He didn't feel angry, he didn't even feel sad. It was as if all his feelings had drained out of him. He didn't cry again. He lay there all day long on his bed, face to the wall. He didn't eat because he wasn't hungry. His mum came in and tried to cheer him up. "One day," she told him, "one day, we'll live in a house with a proper garden. Then we can have a dog. Promise."

"But it won't be Best Mate, will it?" he said.

A little later his dad came in and sat on his bed. He tried something different. "After what you did," he said, "I reckon you deserve a proper treat. We'll go to the football tomorrow. Local Derby. We'll have a pizza first, margherita, your favourite. What d'you say?"

Patrick said nothing. "A good night's sleep is what you need," his dad went on. "You'll feel a lot better tomorrow. Promise." Everyone, Patrick thought, was doing an awful lot of promising, and that was always a bad sign.

From up in his room Patrick heard them all evening whispering urgently in the kitchen below – it was loud enough for him to hear almost every word they said. His mum was going on about how she wished they didn't have to live in a flat. "Never mind a dog," she was saying, "Patrick needs a place where he can play out. All kids do. We've been cooped up in this flat all his life."

"It's a nice flat," said his dad. "I like it here."

"Oh, well then, that's fine, I suppose. Let's stay here for ever, shall we?"

"I didn't mean it like that, you know I didn't."

It wasn't a proper row, not even a heated argument. There were no raised voices, but they talked of nothing else all evening.

In the end Patrick bored of it, and anyway he was tired. He kept closing his eyes, and whenever he did he found himself living the day through again, the best of it and the worst of it. It was so easy to let his mind roam, simply to drift away of its own accord. He liked where it was taking him. He could see Best Mate, now a fully grown greyhound, streaking across the park, and he could see himself haring after him, then both of them lying there in the grass, the sun blazing down, with Best Mate stretched out beside him, his paw on his arm and gazing lovingly at him out of his wide brown eyes. Patrick fell asleep dreaming of that moment, of Best Mate looking up at him, and even when he woke up he found himself dreaming exactly the same thing. And that was strange, Patrick thought, very strange indeed.

Best Mate was still lying there beside him, only somehow he looked much smaller than he had before, and they weren't outside in the park in the sunshine, and his nose was cold and wet. Patrick knew that because Best Mate was suddenly snuffling at Patrick's ear, licking it, then crawling on top of him and licking his nose as well. That

was when he first dared to hope that this was all just too life-like to be a dream, that it might be real, really real. He looked up. His mum and dad were standing there grinning down at him like a couple of cats that had got the cream. The radio was on down in the kitchen, the kettle was whistling and the toast was burning. He *was* awake. This was happening! It was a true and actual happening!

"Mum rang up the rescue centre last night," his dad was telling him, "and I went and fetched him home first thing this morning. Are you happy now?"

"Happy," said Patrick.

"A lot, or a little?" his dad asked.

"A lot," Patrick said.

"And by the way, Patrick," his mum was saying as they went to the door, "your dad and me, we've been talking. We thought having a dog might make us get on and really do it."

"Do what?"

"Get a proper house with a little bit of a garden. We should have done it a long time ago."

And that was when the giggling started, partly

 41

because Best Mate was sitting down on Patrick's chest now, snuffling in his ear, but mostly because he had never been so happy in all his life.

That same morning – it was a Saturday – they went out and bought a basket for Best Mate, a basket big enough for him to grow into, a bright red lead, a dog bowl and some dog food, and a little collar too with a brass disc hanging from it, engraved with his name and their phone number, just in case Best Mate ever got himself lost. In the afternoon they all walked up the hill through the iron gate and into the park, with Best Mate all tippy-toed and pulling on his lead. Once by the bench at the top of the hill Patrick and Best Mate ran off on their own, down to the pond where they scared the ducks silly, and then back up through the trees to the bench where his mum and dad were waiting. It was better than footie, bike riding, skate-boarding, kite-flying, better than all of them put together. And afterwards they lay down on the crisp autumn leaves exhausted, and Best Mate gazed up into Patrick's eyes just as he had in the dream, so that Patrick had to squeeze his eyes tight shut and then open them again just to be quite sure that the whole day had really happened.

Best Mate grew up fast, no longer a cute and clumsy puppy, but a creature of astonishing beauty and grace and power, known and loved all over the park. Within the year they had found the small house they were looking for, with a walled garden at the back. It was nearer the park, but a little further away from school. That didn't matter. Patrick's dad dropped him off at the canal bridge as he always had done, and he'd walk along the tow-path past the sweet and sour smelling brown sauce factory and up the tow-path steps to the road, where Bossy Boots would be waiting with his lollipop stick.

Ever since Mr Boots had told his fib about helping him out of the canal that day, Patrick had always done his best to avoid him. But he had to cross the road every day, and when he did Mr Boots was always waiting, ready with some feeble joke or other about what had happened. "No dogs in the canal today, Patrick?" or "No early morning swim. Patrick?" And every time he'd laugh like a drain as he ushered him across the road.

In school they still talked about "The Great Puppy Rescue". They'd all written stories about it and painted pictures too. These were still up on the wall in the front hall with all the sports cups and the school photographs, along with a cutting from the front page of the local newspaper, laminated and in big print so that everyone could easily read it. "Patrick's Puppy Plunge" was the banner headline, and above it there was a photo of Patrick with Best Mate in his arms, with Mr Boots and Mrs Brightwell on either side of him, and a dozen other children around them, all grinning into the camera – except for Jimmy Rington, who wasn't exactly glowering, but wasn't smiling much either.

So the hero-glow hung around Patrick all that year, which of course he quite liked. No one called him "loser" any more. No one laughed at him any more. So sometimes he even looked forward to school these days. The little greyhound had changed his whole life around, at school and at home. Best Mate was always there with his mum to meet him when he came out of school every afternoon. So everyone got to cuddle and pet him. Maybe this was why the legend of The Great Puppy Rescue was not forgotten – after all Best Mate was there to remind them of it every day. All the teachers seemed to love him too. Mrs Brightwell in particular made a great fuss of him and Patrick loved that – it made him feel very special.

What he didn't like so much was that Bossy Boots was now making out that he'd jumped into the canal himself to help rescue Best Mate. Worse still he was always trying to persuade Patrick's mum to race him, that he was too good a greyhound to be kept at home just as a pet. He told everyone that Best Mate had champion written all over him. This of course only added to the sparkle of the legend, and it was a legend that was changing. The star of the legend had been Patrick at first, but it was Best Mate who was the star now. Patrick didn't mind this in the least. On the contrary, as far as he was concerned Best Mate had always been the star. Every time Patrick came out of the school gates and saw him waiting there for him he felt so proud.

Stories went around the school – spread mostly by Mr Boots – of how Best Mate had been seen running up on the park at full stretch, how no one had ever seen a dog run that fast. Everyone knew that Patrick and Best Mate had become completely inseparable, how Patrick never needed to put him on a lead any more, nor muzzle him; how he'd walk close beside Patrick down the street, his cheek touching Patrick's leg. As faithful and fond as a guide dog, Best Mate was instantly protective, and even fearsome if he ever felt that anyone, dog or human, might be a threat to Patrick. The gentle eyes would flash, the hackles go up along his neck and back, and every muscle in his body would be suddenly tense and taut, ready to spring. But it took only a word or a glance from Patrick to calm him down at once. They spent so much time together that each seemed to understand the other instinctively by now, so much so that up in the park it was hardly ever necessary for Patrick to whistle for Best Mate, or call him back. He just came of his own accord.

At home and at school everyone could see how

happy Patrick had become since the day of The Great Puppy Rescue. "Less anxious, less isolated, more outgoing, more confident," Mrs Brightwell had written in her school report. And it was true. Patrick laughed more these days, joined in more. Every story he wrote in his literacy class somehow managed to involve a dog, usually a greyhound. But Mr Butterworth didn't mind. Patrick was writing pages and pages these days, instead of just a scrappy paragraph or two. In most of the pictures he painted, you could find a greyhound somewhere. And his bedroom wall was covered with pictures and photographs of Best Mate.

Patrick spent every hour of his spare time and all his pocket money on him. He'd bring home chews or biscuits for him, whenever he went to the shops. He polished his name disc so that it gleamed, groomed him every evening, and even cleaned his teeth for him sometimes, so his breath wouldn't smell. He'd make sure his food was just how Best Mate wanted it, but he would never stay to watch him eat it, because he knew Best Mate liked to do this in private. So he'd give him a pat and leave him to it. No one minded at all that Patrick had become one-track minded, because he was so obviously happy.

Settled now in the new house, Best Mate had long since outgrown his basket – they had completely miscalculated how big and tall he was going to grow. But they didn't need to get another one, because he now occupied the sofa. A "giraffe-dog" Patrick's dad called him. His mum didn't mind too much because he was a clean-living dog. He left no hairs behind him, and brought very little dirt in from the garden or back from the park. He did bury his bones sometimes under the cushions on the sofa, but Patrick usually found those and got rid of them before his mum discovered them.

Best Mate would lie there quite happily on the sofa for most of the day waiting to fetch Patrick home from school, longing for his daily run in the park. They'd walk together up to their favourite bench, right at the top of the park. From there

Patrick could watch Best Mate run, whichever way he went. Once into his stride this "giraffe-dog" would be transformed into a "cheetah-dog", and people would simply stand and stare as he streaked away into the distance. From time to time other dogs would try to chase him, try to keep up, but none of them had the speed nor the stamina to stay with him for long. He could outrun and outsmart all of them. He could jink like a gazelle, bound like a springbok. And Patrick was always waiting for him by the bench when he came back.

Every time Patrick watched him run he could feel his whole body warming to the roots of his hair with the sheer thrill of it. And whenever Best Mate came haring back to him over the park, Patrick was filled with a surge of such pride and joy that he felt like whooping with exultation, which he very often did. Best Mate would stand at his side then resting for a while, leaning into him, his nose searching out Patrick's hand for comfort and reassurance. But sooner or later he'd see a terrier scampering past, or a crow landing nearby, or a squirrel's tail twitching in the grass, and he'd be off like a rocket again. Patrick knew it was the chase he loved best, but just the chase. He never used his great teeth for killing. They were for smiling with only, but the crows and the squirrels didn't know that.

More than once Mr Boots came up to the park to watch Best Mate go through his paces. He'd take photographs of him too, and Patrick didn't like that. He thought Bossy Boots should ask him first, but he never did. Some of Patrick's friends from school would be up there too sometimes, playing football, Jimmy Rington as well. But whenever Best Mate got into his stride, they'd very soon stop playing and just stand there and stare. Like Patrick, they would all be holding their breath in awe as Best Mate fairly flew over the ground. It was powerful, it was beautiful, it was wonderful.

But the day it happened – Best Mate must have been about eighteen months old by now – the two of them were almost alone together in the park. That was because it was later than usual, almost evening by the time they got there. Patrick's mum had made him stay in to finish his homework first. So Patrick wasn't in a very good mood and grumbled about it to Best Mate all the way up the hill to the park. He cheered up though when he saw the swallows were back and skimming over the grass. He loved to watch them, and he knew Best Mate loved to chase them. So it was strange when, instead of taking off after them, Best Mate stayed by his side, looking up at him and licking his lips nervously.

"Off you go, boy," Patrick said. "What's the matter with you? Go on! Go, go, go!"

But Best Mate didn't move. There was a low growl in the back of his throat, which was very unlike him. His ears were laid back on his head, and his whole body was trembling.

"It's all right," Patrick told him, stroking his neck to calm him. "It's just a little darker than usual, that's all. Nothing to worry about. Lots of smells to chase. Off you go." He bent down and kissed him on top of his head. "You'll be fine, promise. Go on! Go, go, go!"

Best Mate looked to him once more for reassurance. At that moment a swallow swooped down over their heads, and skimmed away over the grass – it was as if he was teasing Best Mate, taunting him. Best Mate didn't hesitate. He was gone, gathering speed with every bounding stride, his neck straining, following the swallow's every twist and turn. "You're so beautiful," Patrick breathed. Then he shouted it out so that the entire world could hear. "You're beautiful! Beautiful!" He watched Best Mate racing away down the hill and then disappearing into the trees. It was the way he often went, his favourite run. He'd circle the lake at the bottom, scatter the ducks, scare the geese, and come running back through the trees, pounding up the hill towards Patrick. A few minutes later, Best Mate still hadn't come back. That was a little unusual, but Patrick wasn't worried. Best Mate might have got himself a bit lost in the gathering gloom, he thought. So he whistled for him, and called him. But he didn't come and didn't come, and now Patrick knew something had to be wrong. All his worst fears jostled in his head. Best Mate was wandering lost through the streets. He'd been run over, stolen, drowned, savaged by another dog, poisoned. However loud Patrick called and whistled no dog came running up the hill towards him through the dusk. He could hear no answering bark, only the distant roar of the traffic.

So Patrick ran down the dark hill, following where Best Mate might have gone, through the trees, around the pond and back up the hill towards the bench, stopping every now and again to call for him and listen and look. He couldn't whistle any more by now because he was crying too much. He saw no one in the park, no dogs, only shadowy ducks and geese cruising out on the dark water of the pond.

Patrick realised then that he needed help. He ran all the way home. His mum and dad came at once. The three of them searched the park with torches all night long, called and called until they knew it was pointless to go on any longer. It was dawn by the time they got home, all of them hoping against hope that Best Mate had found his own way back. He hadn't. Patrick sat at the bottom of the stairs with his head in his hands, while his dad phoned the Police. They took a description of Best Mate and said they would do their best to keep an eye out for him. They'd call back if they found him. No call came.

A further search of the park by daylight only made things worse for Patrick. Everyone else's dog was up there bounding around, scampering through the grass, fetching sticks and balls and frisbees. Patrick told everyone, asked everyone. No one had seen Best Mate. It was as if he had simply vanished off the face of the earth.

*   *   *

Muzzled and caged in the back of a van, I had long hours to think about everything that had happened to me that evening on the park, about how stupid and gullible I had been to allow myself to get caught. And then there were more long, dark hours to remember how happy my life had been before I was so suddenly snatched away from everyone and everything I loved. The memories of it all kept repeating themselves in my head like a recurring nightmare I longed to wake from, but could not. I was trapped inside this nightmare, and could see no possible way of ever escaping from it.

In the van there was pitch black all around me. I had no idea whether it was night or day, no idea where I was being taken, only that I was a prisoner, that with every hour that passed I was being driven further and further away from home and from Patrick. I had tried yelping and barking, tried scratching at the door. Now I lay there curled up in my misery, exhausted and dejected, the van shaking and rattling around me. I closed my eyes and tried to think myself home, to blot out the terror I was living through, tried to make myself believe that I was back on the sofa at home with Patrick, that none of this had happened. But that was when the nightmare would begin, and I would have to live through everything that had happened all over again.

Patrick had finished his homework. He came over to the sofa and stroked me just where I liked it best, under my chest, which for some reason made one of my back legs kick out involuntarily. Patrick giggled. I think he loved doing it as much as I loved him doing it. Then he was putting my coat on me, and we were out of the warmth of the house and into the street, trotting together up the hill and through the gate to the park. This was the moment I longed for every day, to be out there with Patrick. Soon I'd be in the park and running, running, running, but I'd never set off till he gave me the word.

Patrick always had to speak the words first. "Off you go, boy," he'd whisper. "Go on! Go, go, go!" I didn't really need telling. I was just waiting for him to say it. When I ran, I ran for the sheer pleasure of the chase, to feel the spring in my legs and the power surging through me, to feel the wind, to scatter the crows, to leave all the other dogs far behind me. But I ran for Patrick too, because I knew he was there watching me, and that the faster I ran the more he'd be loving it, and the more he loved it, the more I did too. Coming out of the trees and back up the hill towards him I'd put on my best show, lengthening with every stride, because I could feel his pride in my running, and his love for me as I came up to him, as he smoothed my neck. That was the best moment of all, when both of us were jubilant together, exultant together.

But this evening, I didn't want to run. Even when he said the words I didn't want to go. In the end I ran only because Patrick wanted me to. It wasn't just the dark that worried me, though it's true I've always been rather nervous of the dark. It was a feeling I had deep inside me that there was some kind of danger lurking out there in the park, that I'd be safer if I stayed with Patrick. Maybe it was also because there weren't any other dogs about, I don't know. I did wonder why they weren't there. I did think too that running wouldn't be so much fun without a dog or two to race against. I could chase the swallows, and I loved that, but it wasn't quite the same. They weren't company. Besides, I could never beat them. To be honest I never even got near them, but that didn't stop me trying.

Anyway, once I was off and into my running I forgot all that, forgot all my worries. I raced away from Patrick, away down the hill towards the pond. There were two men standing there beside a white van, and one of them I recognised at once. In fact I wasn't at all surprised to see Mr Boots. He was often there on the heath watching me. I'd seen him a few times down by the pond just recently, another man with him. They'd be watching me through binoculars, like Patrick's dad sometimes did.

They were both there this time too, and this time, as he had once or twice before, Mr Boots whistled me over. I went because I liked him. I liked him because he always gave me a biscuit, and I can never resist

biscuits. He'd never done me any harm. When I went up to him he patted me and I waited for my biscuit. He gave me one, but as I ate it he reached out suddenly, grabbed me by my collar, and held on to me. I thought that was odd, because he hadn't done that before, and it all became stranger still when my head began to swim, and my legs buckled underneath me. I found myself lying down at his feet then, Mr Boots holding me fast on the ground, not that I could have struggled anyway. I had no strength left for that.

"Don't you worry," Mr Boots was saying. "He's right out of it. He couldn't hurt a fly."

"You haven't given him too much stuff, have you?" said the other voice.

"'Course not," Mr Boots told him. "I know what I'm about, don't I? He'll be right as rain in an hour or two, you'll see."

"He'd better be," said the other. "I'm getting out of here before that ruddy kid comes looking for him." He was undoing my collar now. "Here, you'd better lose this, chuck it in the pond. I won't be needing his phone number, will I? Nor his name."

"What about my money?" Mr Boots asked. "£500 was the deal."

They argued loudly about it for some time. "£400, take it or leave it."

Then Mr Boots was shouting at him: "That's robbery that is, daylight bleeding robbery!"

"That's rich coming from you, Bootsy," said the other, "from a dog thief. And mind you get rid of that collar."

They were still arguing as they put a muzzle on me, tight, so tight that it hurt. I heard Mr Boots storming off, swearing and cursing as he went. Then I was dumped in the back of a van, and the door slammed after me. I drifted in and out of sleep for some time, I think, before waking up properly, before I really understood that my nightmare had been no dream, that everything was true, that I was not home again on the sofa with Patrick.

It was not the cold nor the blackness all around me that frightened me most, that made me tremble and whimper as I lay there. It was the fear of the unknown that truly terrified me. Where was I being taken to? Why had they done this? What was going to happen to me? Would I ever see Patrick again?

"Be Fast, Brighteyes,
Be Very Fast"

For Becky the only good days were when Craig wasn't at home, and she wasn't at school. So that Sunday morning had been a good day, so far, just her and her mother alone together, like it used to be three years ago, before they'd moved out of town and come to live out on the moor miles away from all her friends and so much that she had known and loved. It wasn't that she didn't like being in the countryside. She did, when Craig wasn't there, and when she could get away on her own. She'd ride out on Red to the top of High Moor, galloping most of the way. Once up there she'd clamber up on the rocks and stand there leaning into the wind, revelling in it.

This was her place, her rock, the only place she could talk to her father, tell him everything. His spirit was in the wind, she was sure of it, in the air she breathed up there, in the rocks themselves. He was as real to her as the wild moorland ponies, the browsing cattle and the shifting sheep. It was a place of rising larks and wheeling buzzards in the summer, of wind-buffeted crows in the winter. Whatever the season, Becky knew her father was always there with her, always listening, and that soothed, for a while at least, the aching loneliness inside her. And that was also why she loved being around the kennels with the greyhounds. They got her out of the house and away from Craig, and they were her friends too. They listened and they understood.

Becky and her mother had been working together around the kennels all that morning, feeding the greyhounds and exercising them, bedding up the calves and the lambing ewes in the farm yard. They hadn't argued at all, and that was because Craig was not around, and because they hadn't even talked about him. If he wasn't there and he wasn't mentioned, they were fine together. Craig had left the night before in his van. He was going to fetch another dog, a top dog, a sure-fire champion, he said. So for a while at least Becky and her mother had been left to themselves. All the kennel work was done and the two of them were mucking out Red's stable together. Becky was singing away to herself as she shook out the straw, while her mother tossed the hay up into the rack.

"I wish you were always this happy," said her mother.

"I would be," Becky replied, "if it wasn't for him."

"If it wasn't for him, Becky, we wouldn't be here. You should remember that sometimes. We came from a pokey little room with a bathroom the size of a postage stamp – have you forgotten? And now we've got all this, the farmhouse, the moor, Red, the dogs, everything."

"So I suppose I have to be grateful, do I?" Becky could feel the anger in her rising. She tried to hold it back. "We were all right before, Mum, when there was just the two of us. We had all we needed."

"Listen, Becky, I really don't want to argue with you," said her mother. "I just want you to try a little harder to like him, for my sake. I mean, the minute he walks in you go out, and you hardly ever speak to him."

"That's because I've got nothing to say." Becky was tearful already. "Nothing he'd want to hear, anyway. I mean, what do you want me to do, Mum? Do you want me to tell him what I really think of him? Do you? 'Listen up, Craig, you bully my mother, make her cook for you, clean for you, work like a slave on your farm – me too when I'm not at school – and you never do any work yourself. Tell me Craig, when did you last clean out the kennels? Oh yes, and another thing, why do you put me down all the time? Either I'm a "stroppy teenager" or a "spoilt brat", or I'm "dressed up like a Barbie doll". Excuse me, Craig, what business is it of yours, and how come you keep telling me what to do anyway? I mean just who do you think you are? You're not my father.'"

She paused for breath and calmed down a little. "Come on, Mum," she went on. "You know all he thinks about is money and betting and racing his greyhounds. And do you know what? He doesn't even like the dogs. And what's more he doesn't even want me to like them. He does all he can to stop me. 'Don't pet them,' he says. 'Bad for them,' he says. 'They're racing dogs, athletes, not poodles, not pets.' He just uses them up, Mum, and when they don't make him any more money, when they don't win, he just gets rid of them. I've tried, Mum. I really have. I just wish you'd never met him, that's all. I don't know what you see in him. I really don't."

Becky knew her tirade had gone too far, that she'd spoilt the day, that it would make her mother cry, and that she'd hate herself later for making her unhappy again. But to her surprise, her mother didn't cry this time. Instead she went very quiet.

"You don't understand," said her mother after a while. "He was good to me, kind to me. We had fun together. I needed some fun."

"Didn't last though, did it, Mum?"

Her mother didn't reply. For a few moments she just busied herself filling up the water buckets. Then she went on. "It's not all bad though, is it, Becky? At least you've got the dogs. You love the dogs, don't you?"

"Of course I do."

"Well then. And we've still got each other. How does the song go? *Always Look on the Bright Side of Life.*" And they both began to hum it together.

Becky's mother smiled across at her then, and Becky knew there was a lot she was saying in that smile, maybe that she didn't entirely disagree with much of what Becky had said, but that she just couldn't say it, not yet, maybe not ever. The dogs were suddenly barking from the kennels across the yard. That was when they both heard the van come crunching down the farm track, and rattle over the cattle grid into the yard. They looked at one another, and Becky knew then that her mum was dreading his return as much as she was. Craig was back.

They looked on from the stable door as Craig slipped a choke-chain around the dog's neck, and hauled him out of the back of the van – Craig was never gentle with his dogs. That was when he

caught sight of them. "Well, what d'you think? Smart dog, eh? Looks the part, doesn't he? He may be a bit small at the moment, but he'll grow. He goes like the wind, I'm telling you. I got him cheap too. Few months time, and he could be as fast as Alfie, maybe faster." The dog tried to escape, but Craig jerked on the chain and yanked him back. "Come here, you little beggar you! You see. He can't wait to get running. It's what he's made for. You know what you're looking at? A champion. I mean it. This one is the real thing. He is going to win and win. And that means money, lots of it. You'll see."

The greyhound, light fawn with a small white patch on his chest, stood there trembling at the end of his chain, looking about him nervously. "Here Becky!" Craig waved her over. "Don't just stand there gawping. Get over here. Put him in with Alfie. I want Alfie to teach him everything he knows about racing. And you'd better give him something to eat while you're about it. Which reminds me. What's for lunch? I'm starving."

Becky hesitated very deliberately. She objected to being bossed about, and wanted him to know it. So she took her time, leaning the dung fork against the wall, and then wandering very slowly across the yard towards him, staring him out as she came. She disliked everything about him, his loudness and his brashness, how he always had to be the centre of attention. She hated looking at him even, so she tried not to. He wasn't ugly or gross, it wasn't that. It was just that he always looked so full of himself.

"Well, take your time, why don't you?" He said, handing her the chain. "And no spoiling him, you hear me? None of your namby pamby nonsense." Becky knew exactly what was coming next. "He's a racing dog, an athlete, not a poodle, not a pet."

"What's he called?" Becky asked him.

"Call him whatever you like. Just look after him."

Moments later Becky found herself alone in the yard with the new dog. As she walked him towards the kennels all the other dogs, all fourteen of them, had their noses through the

 77

bars, scrutinising the newcomer, some of them up on their hind legs and yelping in excitement. Becky laughed. "Don't you know it's rude to stare?" she told them.

She crouched down by Alfie's kennel so that she could introduce them properly through the kennel gate, so they could get to know one another slowly. Alfie was a giant of a greyhound, black and white with a slightly greying muzzle.

"Meet Alfie," she said, reaching through the bars to stroke his ears. "He's the fastest dog we've got, aren't you, Alfie? Won sixty-two out of eighty races, haven't you? A real champion. But I'm not supposed to stroke you, am I? I do though, don't I? I pet them all because I like it, and because they like it. Alfie and me, we're very special friends, aren't we, Alfie? We go up on the moor together with Red, don't we? Long walks, long talks."

She felt the new dog shivering and shaking

against her leg. He was terrified or cold, or both. "Don't you worry. Alfie won't hurt you." She took his face in her hands then and looked deep into his eyes. "So what am I going to call you? You've got to have a name. Can't not have a name, can you? You've got one already, I bet. Every dog's got a name. I wonder what yours is. Wish you could tell me." She thought for some moments, and then it came to her. "Brighteyes. That'll do. You'll be Brighteyes. How d'you like that? Craig'll give you some stupid racing name... 'Bucks Fizz' or 'Speedy Gonzalez'. And down at the track they'll give you a number – they always do. But here you'll be Brighteyes." She kissed him on his head and whispered: "Be fast, Brighteyes, be very fast, and they won't take you away from me. Never forget that."

Becky stayed there watching the two dogs for some time, Alfie circling Brighteyes, checking him out, and all the while Brighteyes stood in the

middle of the kennel trembling from head to tail.
After a few minutes Alfie seemed satisfied,
because he came and stood alongside him then,
very close, their shoulders touching. Becky could
see that the two of them were friends already.
Alfie stood almost a head higher. He was resting
his chin on Brighteyes' neck, and this must have
been a great comfort to Brighteyes because very
soon the trembling stopped altogether.

Within days it was as if they had known
each other all their lives. They'd become quite
inseparable. Whenever Becky let them out
Brighteyes would stick to Alfie like a shadow.

Very soon she was so confident Brighteyes wouldn't run off that she was able to take both dogs with her when she went out riding on Red, something she liked to do as often as she could. That first morning she took them out together, they raced way ahead of her, almost side by side, but always Alfie leading by a neck and Brighteyes following. However fast Becky rode, they raced ahead faster, hurdling the rocks and streams, pausing only to let her catch up.

They ended up on the very top of High Moor. The dogs sat beside one another next to her on the bank, their panting almost synchronised, as Red grazed the grass busily below, scarcely ever lifting his head. The dogs were both looking at her quizzically. "You're right," she told them. "Dad's up here, isn't he? You know it too, don't you? This is my favourite place in the whole wide world, because Dad's here, because I feel free. That's why you like it too. You love to run free.

It's what you were made for. You weren't made for that horrible dog track. This is where you belong, like I do."

In fact, Becky had hardly ever been to see the greyhounds racing. The few times she had gone she'd hated every minute of it. She loathed having to watch the dogs she knew and loved treated simply as numbered racing machines, so many of them quite evidently terrified by all the bright lights and the noise of the crowd, of the blaring loud speakers, and the deafening music. Beside them in the stand, Craig would bellow and roar, whether his dogs won or not. It didn't matter if it was a winning triumph or a losing disaster. Either way he'd go berserk, and then afterwards he'd drink too much with his cronies, while Becky and her mother and the dogs had to sit and wait in the car park for him.

On the way home, especially if he'd lost heavily on the dogs or the betting, he'd start shouting at her mother, and if Becky tried to intervene he'd turn on her too. Craig could be very frightening at times like these, and Becky didn't want to be near him. So, more often than not, she'd tell her mother she had homework to finish, which was sometimes true, and stay at home. She'd make sure she was in bed with the lights out by the time they got back. She could tell right away at breakfast the next morning whether the dogs had won or not, whether Craig had lost money. If he'd had a bad night, he'd sit there in an angry and sullen silence. He'd start nasty and he'd stay nasty all day. Neither Becky nor her mother were allowed to forget it. He'd snap at them and find fault with everything they said or did. So Becky certainly preferred it when the dogs won.

But there was another reason why she always wanted the dogs to win. It had taken a while for her to grasp what was really going on. If ever a dog began to lose too often, she knew that sooner or later it would happen. The battered grey Land Rover would come rattling down the farm track into the yard. Whenever it came Becky did her best to stay out of the way. She dreaded it every time. If she asked about it or objected to it, it would send Craig into one of his rages. So, filled with guilt, she'd keep quiet, go to her room and watch from her window.

Craig would usually talk with the driver for a minute or two. Becky hadn't ever really seen his face properly. Most of it was hidden by a flat cap. He wore dirty blue overalls, and shuffled rather than walked over to the kennels. Every time the chosen dog was hauled out of his kennel, Becky could see that he understood what was going to happen to him, because he'd fight against it, pulling on his chain, desperately trying to break free. The other dogs seemed to sense it too. They'd set up a plaintive chorus of yelping and whining that lasted long after the Land Rover had disappeared up the track.

Becky asked her mother again and again where the dogs were being taken to, and who the man in the dirty blue overalls was. Her mother couldn't say much about it, and that was what was so worrying for Becky. All her mother would tell her was that once a greyhound's racing days were over, he was taken off to an animal rescue centre, and from there they went to good homes where they'd be well looked after. But then often she'd add something that Becky had never been able to believe. "Craig's very generous," she'd tell her. "He gives the rescue centre a big donation every time they take a dog away. He's good like that – you just don't see that side of him, you never have. You mustn't worry so much." But Becky did worry, because she was quite sure by now that Craig didn't have a generous bone in his body, that her mother seemed completely blind to how Craig really was, how he felt about his dogs, and how ruthless he was with them.

To Becky, who had spent so much time with the greyhounds, it was all utterly heartless and cruel, an outrage. Every time she had to watch them being dragged away like that, just because they could not longer win races, made her hate Craig even more. He never warned her when it was going to happen, nor which of them was going to be taken off next in the battered grey Land Rover, never to be seen again. So she never had the chance to say goodbye properly. She dreaded that one day Alfie might stop winning, might just get too old for it, might injure himself, and then he'd be taken away too. She knew that one day it was going to happen. It was just a question of time. Brighteyes was younger of course. Maybe he had a longer future, but their futures always ended the same way.

It was something her mother said to her one evening when they were alone that changed Becky's mind about going along with them to the races. "You handle the dogs so much better than I do, Becky," she said. "They know you better. They like you better. I've watched you with them. They run like the wind when you're around. They always win more. I know they do. And besides," she went on, "it'll make Craig happy to see you take more of an interest. And I'd like it too, to have you there, I mean. You'd be company for me."

Becky thought about it for a long time. Craig was entering Brighteyes for more and more races these days, trying him out, testing him, always with Alfie. Becky hated watching them being driven off in the van. She missed them when they were gone. It was that more than anything that changed her mind. She wanted to be with them all she could. And if her mother was right, maybe she really could help Alfie and the others run faster and keep winning. That was enough for Becky. She'd go. She'd ignore Craig, just pretend he wasn't there.

The journeys to the dog tracks on race nights were long and tedious, all the way to London sometimes, to Walthamstow for the big races, and Craig was his usual boorish and beastly self every time. But it did cheer her mother up to have her there, and anyway Becky usually managed to keep her distance from Craig. She was always in the back of the van with the dogs, happy just to be with them. The evenings she looked forward to most were when Alfie and Brighteyes were running – Craig liked to run them together. He had put them through their paces every day up on the moor behind the house. They could all see how the older dog was bringing the younger one on every time they ran, how quick and strong Brighteyes was becoming, improving with every race, how he would never let Alfie get away from him, but stuck to his shoulder all the time, like an unshakeable shadow.

In race after race all over the country they came in first and second, usually but not always Alfie crossing the line first by just a whisker. It was a winning streak which went on for nearly a year. Craig could not believe his luck – he'd never before raked in so much prize money, nor so many trophies for the sideboard back at the farmhouse. He was doing just as well out of his

betting too. But all the while other dogs in the kennels came and went. Every couple of months or so Becky saw the battered grey Land Rover come rattling down the farm track. She wept

every time it happened. She just hoped, and now she prayed too, that Alfie and Brighteyes would go on winning for ever and never have to be taken away.

By this time the two dogs were quite inseparable. Try to take one out of the kennel and not the other, and they would both make a terrible fuss, an ear-splitting hullabaloo of yowling and whining and yapping that upset every dog in the kennels. Brighteyes stood as tall as Alfie these days, though he was not as powerfully muscled. For each other, and for Becky too, they had become soul mates. She would never go without them when she rode out on Red. And if ever Craig and her mother went out and left her alone in the house for an evening, she would bring them in from the kennels. She liked to let them have the run of the house, to jump up on the sofa beside her. It was strictly against Craig's rules to have any of the dogs inside the house, but Craig's rules were of no account to Becky when he wasn't there.

She loved these evenings, just the three of them with the log fire blazing and her music on. She'd often find herself talking to them, confiding in them all her deepest thoughts. She was lying there one evening with Alfie and Brighteyes sprawled beside her on the sofa, when she began to feel all her pent-up grief welling inside her, until she was so utterly overwhelmed by waves of sadness that the whole story came pouring out of her, about her father, about what had happened on that terrible Sunday morning nearly three years before. It was a secret she had never shared with anyone before, not even her mother, a secret that had haunted her every day since.

"Whichever way you look at it," she told them, through her tears, "it was my fault. I made it happen. I was the one who had two mugs of hot chocolate the night before and finished all the milk. That was why there was no milk for breakfast. Mum was away visiting Nan, who hadn't been too well. Before Nan died, she got this emphysema thing. She couldn't breathe very well and she used to get panicky. So sometimes

 95

Mum went over to be with her at weekends. That's why there was just Dad and me at home, and I'm lying in bed upstairs trying my best not to wake up. Dad shouts up to me and says we've run out of milk, and will I get up and fetch some from the corner shop down the road, while he does the breakfast. But I'm really sleepy and just not feeling like getting up at all, so I pretend I'm still asleep and I haven't heard him.

"The next thing I know I hear the front door open and he's calling upstairs, all jokey and sarcastic. 'I'll go myself then, shall I, Sleepyhead? Oh, and don't you worry yourself about your poor old dad. He doesn't mind going out in the rain and getting himself a good soaking just because his daughter's pigged out on the hot chocolate again last night. You have a nice lie-in, why don't you? Back soon!'

"And then he's gone, and I snuggle down the bed again, feeling a little bit guilty, but not that much, and before I know it I'm dropping off to sleep again. I don't know how long I'm asleep, but it's the front door bell that wakes me. So I go downstairs, a bit fed up, thinking that Dad's forgotten his key accidentally on purpose, just to get me out of bed, and there's the police standing there, two of them, one woman, one man, and they're both looking as if they don't quite know what to say. Then the policeman asks me if my mum's in, and I tell him that Dad'll be back soon, that he's just gone down the shop for some milk. I see them looking at one another, and the policeman takes off his cap and asks if they can come in for a moment.

"That's the first time I think something's wrong – it's just the way they look at each other. But they won't say what it is, nor who they want, nor what the matter is. They just ask where Mum has gone and they say they'd like to speak to her, so I give them her mobile number. The policeman goes out and leaves me with this policewoman who tries to smile at me and make conversation, but she can't do either, not really. So we're just sitting there, the two of us – it seems like for hours – while he's phoning up and stuff, and still Dad doesn't come back and doesn't come back, and I'm wondering why, and knowing by now that something really bad must have happened to him, or maybe to Mum. I keep asking what's going on, but she won't say.

"Then Mum comes in and I can see she's been crying, and she takes me upstairs and we sit on the bed together, and she tells me. It was a lorry that did it, ran out of control at the bottom of the hill, mounted the pavement outside the shop just when Dad was coming out with the milk. But it wasn't the lorry that killed him. It was me, using up all the milk to make my hot chocolate, me staying in bed when he asked me to go."

All the time Becky was talking the dogs' eyes never left her face. "I've never talked about it to anyone else, except Dad of course. I've talked to him lots of times, up on High Moor, and he's all right about it. He says it wasn't my fault, but then he would say that, wouldn't he? Because he wants me to feel better about it. He told me I should tell Mum, that she won't be upset, and just to get on with my life. But I can't forget it, and I can't tell Mum either, because I know she'll hate me for ever, like I hate myself. And anyway, I don't reckon Mum thinks about Dad that much any more, not with Craig around. She hardly ever talks about him. Sometimes I think she's deliberately trying to forget him. Maybe it's the only way she can put up with horrible Craig. She doesn't even like me talking about him, says it upsets Craig.

"'So what?' I say.

"'We've got to move on,' she says – she's always saying that. 'What's happened has happened. We've got to put it behind us. No use crying over spilt milk.'

"She really did say that once, honest. I think of it all the time, the spilt milk on the pavement outside the shop. I never saw it, but I think of it and I wish I didn't. I so want to tell her everything just like I've told you, but I can't, I just can't. And I don't think I ever will."

Becky cried herself to sleep soon afterwards, and her mother and Craig found her still sleeping there on the sofa when they came back, Alfie and Brighteyes lolling beside her, their heads on her lap.

Craig wasn't just angry, he was apoplectic. "If you want to sleep with them," he was yelling right in her face, "then you know what you can do, you can ruddy well go and sleep in the kennels. But you're not going to do it in my house, you get me?"

Her mother tried her best to intervene on Becky's behalf, but that only made things worse. "There you go again," he was yelling at her mother now. "Always taking her side, letting her do what she likes. That's why she's like she is, can't you see? Her dad may have let her run wild and do what she liked. But this is my house and I make the rules here. She knows the rules. No dogs in the house. I've told her often enough, haven't I? And what does she do? She goes and sneaks them in when our backs are turned. And I wouldn't mind betting this isn't the first time either. If she wants to live here, she does what I say, simple as that. Are you hearing me, Becky?"

Becky looked him right in the eye. Anger gave her the courage she needed to answer him back. "I don't want to live here," she shouted at him, "I never did. I hate this house, and I hate you. And if you want me to sleep in the kennels with the dogs, that's fine. I'll sleep in the kennels. I'm not bothered. I don't mind. See if I care." And without another word she slammed out of the house, Alfie and Brighteyes following her across the yard.

A little later her mother came out and tried to persuade her to come back inside the house, to patch things up, and say sorry to Craig. But Becky wouldn't do it.

"I didn't think so," said her mother sadly, "which is why I've brought you out your duvet and a pillow."

So Becky spent that night curled up with the dogs at the back of their kennel, covered in her duvet and sharing a pillow with Brighteyes. And whenever Becky woke, which was often, he'd be there, awake and looking straight back at her. It was Brighteyes who helped her through the night, soothed her anger, and kept her warm.

The bitterness of that row blew over in the end, as all the others had. But the memory of it added to the growing residue of cold resentment between them. Despite all Becky's mother tried to do to maintain some kind of peace between them, the house became more and more a place of sullen silence. When she wasn't at school Becky spent as much time as she could up on the moor with Red and the two dogs, riding each time further and further away from the farm. Time and again she thought of riding off with them and never coming back. It was only the thought of how much it would upset her mother that prevented her from actually doing it.

But of course, whether she liked it or not, the three of them were still thrown together on the evenings when they went off to the dog races. For a while Alfie and Brighteyes kept on winning, one or other of them, regularly enough. But Becky could see, as everyone could, that things were gradually changing. More and more it was Brighteyes who was replacing Alfie as the favourite down at the dog track. He was unquestionably on his way to becoming top dog. Everywhere they went now the cameras were on him, and the bets were on him too.

The two dogs were still just as inseparable as ever, off the track and on it, only now it was Brighteyes who almost always came in first, with Alfie a whisker behind. Alfie was definitely off the pace these days, getting older, everyone said, not past it but certainly past his best. No one could deny he was as eager as ever. His speed out of the traps was electric. In full stride he was still magnificent, but his stamina was failing him. He was having to strain every muscle and sinew to stay with Brighteyes, who, as everyone could plainly see, was coming into his prime.

Down at the track Craig was king of the castle, top trainer, and revelling triumphantly in every moment of it. So long as one of his two champion dogs came first and the other came in second, so long as the prize money was still coming in, and the trophies too, that was all that mattered to Craig. For Becky though every race was a torment. She could see that Alfie was not the dog he had been. He was too tired. He was too old. Every time he ran, she thought it might be his last.

Becky was there at the track the evening Alfie broke down. He looked fine as she led him around the enclosure, full of himself and up on his toes. He was the first out of the traps, as usual, kept tight around the bend and powered ahead, with Brighteyes just behind, but moving up alongside him. It looked to Becky, and to everyone else, like another double win, another one-two. The only question was which of them would finish first. All the other dogs were out of it. Then, with no warning whatever, Alfie simply stopped running, slowed to a limping walk and stood there panting under the glare of the lights, as every other dog streaked by him.

Brighteyes had run on for a few paces when it happened. But then, as he found himself suddenly alone, he slowed, stopped and looked about him.

He saw Alfie standing there alone on the track and came running back towards him. The two famous champions stood side by side on the track, bewildered and alarmed, but still together. By the time Becky had vaulted over the barrier fence on to the track and was running over to them, the whole crowd had fallen silent in the stands. They knew, as Becky did, that they were witnessing the end of a greyhound racing legend, that they had just seen the great Alfie run his last race.

The vet confirmed what everyone already suspected, that a bone in one of Alfie's hocks had broken. There was nothing that could be done. He might be able to run but he would never race again.

No one spoke in the van on the way home that night. Becky sat in the back with the dogs as usual, with Alfie's head on her lap. She waited until they got back later that night, until they were having a cup of tea in the kitchen, before she said anything. Still no one spoke. She'd been thinking about it all the way home. She had made up her mind to swallow her pride and beg.

"I've never asked you for anything before, have I, Craig?" she began. Craig didn't say anything. He just sat there stirring his tea and gazing into it morosely. "It's about Alfie. I'd really like to keep him. I mean, he's won you all that money, all those cups. He's run his heart out for you every time he's raced, hasn't he? And Brighteyes... if Alfie goes, it'll break his heart, and if he's unhappy then he'll never run his best, will he? I know him. Please Craig, I'll look after him. I promise I will."

The look on Craig's face was as scathing as the tone of his voice. "So now it's 'please Craig' all of a sudden, is it? That makes a change, I suppose. Well let me tell you something for nothing: a racing dog is only worth keeping as long as he can win. You heard what that vet said. Alfie's not even going to be able to race again, let alone win. So he goes, just like the others. He's no different. I run a racing kennels here, right? I don't run a dog's rest home for lame greyhounds. So stop your whinging. He goes. Tomorrow. And there's an end to it."

"He'll go to a good home, Becky. It's all right," her mother said. "They all go to good homes, don't they, Craig?"

"Yeah, yeah," Craig muttered. He took a sip of his tea, then banged the mug down on the table.

"There's no sugar in this," he shouted. "You know I always have sugar." Becky's mother, now clearly upset, pushed the sugar bowl towards him. He spooned the sugar in and stirred it. When he looked up, he saw both of them looking back at him waiting for a proper answer. "Of course they do," he snapped. "Good homes, all of them. I've told you, haven't I?"

"Please. Just this once." Becky would not give up. "Please, Craig. I'll never ask for anything ever again. Let me keep him please."

Craig drank his tea and said nothing for a while. "All right," he replied at last, "I'll think about it."

Becky's mother reached out and put her hand on his. "Thank you," she said, "from both of us." She looked hard at Becky.

"Yes. Thank you," Becky mumbled. It was hardly convincing, but it was the best she was prepared to do.

Early the next morning Becky saddled up Red

in the yard for their morning ride. She wanted to take Alfie and Brighteyes with her as usual, but she could see that Alfie was still carrying his bad leg, hardly able to limp across the kennel. She knew Brighteyes wouldn't want to come without him, so she decided to leave them both behind.

She led Red over to their kennel and crouched down beside them. "It's all right, Alfie," she told him. "I've fixed it with Craig. You're staying. No one's going to take you away. And as soon as your leg's better you can come for a run on the moor. All right?" She smoothed his head and left them. As she rode out of the yard, she turned and saw them both standing there looking after her.

She could tell that Red wasn't happy without the dogs there. He kept stopping, lifting his head and whinnying for them, so it took her much longer than usual to get up to High Moor. She sat on her rock and told her father everything that had happened, how she'd bring the dogs up to see him

again once Alfie was fit. Then, as she was talking, a strange thing happened. A white barn owl came floating out of nowhere, like a passing spirit. She flew away down the valley, harried all the way by a pair of cawing crows. Becky had never before seen a barn owl out in broad daylight like this. A shiver of dread came over her, and she knew it wasn't the cold. She felt it was an omen of some kind, a warning, even a premonition of evil. She mounted up at once and rode hard all the way home.

As she came down off the hill behind the farmhouse Becky heard an engine starting up in the yard below. She recognised it as the engine of a Land Rover. She feared the worst at once, and knew now for sure what the barn owl had been telling her. She saw the battered Land Rover rattling up the track away from the farmyard, and heard from inside it the unmistakable sound of Alfie barking, of Alfie scrabbling at the door in his terror.

As Becky came riding into the yard Brighteyes was up on his hind legs, frantic to get out, yelping and whining. He was alone in his kennel.

Becky didn't confront Craig. She knew that it was too late, that there was no point. It gave her some satisfaction to hear from inside the house the sound of her mother at last standing up to Craig, telling him exactly what she thought of him, but for Becky it was no great comfort. It was too little and too late. She didn't go into the house at all, but spent the rest of the day in the kennel with Brighteyes where she knew she was needed. He was just like he had been when he'd first arrived. He was trembling violently. All day he wouldn't eat and he wouldn't drink, but stood with his head through the bars of the kennel, looking for Alfie, waiting for him.

By the time Becky rode out with Brighteyes the next morning, she still had not managed to get him to eat anything, and he'd drunk next to

113

nothing either. Without Alfie there, Brighteyes never once raced ahead, never bounded away through the bracken like a deer. He loped alongside Becky and Red, his head hanging, all the spring gone from his step. Once up on High Moor he whined wistfully as he looked all about him. Then he came over and sat down beside Becky, his head laid on his paws. He never looked up at her, not once, as if he could not bear to, as if he felt she had betrayed him. She talked to him, stroked him, tried to comfort and reassure him, but he was inconsolable.

"Mum wouldn't lie to me," Becky told him. "So it must be like she said. He's gone to a good home. Alfie's fine. I know he is."

Brighteyes looked up at her then, and she knew absolutely that he did not believe her, that he knew something she didn't know, something dreadful and unthinkable, something he was desperately trying to tell her. Quite suddenly, as she was looking into his eyes, she understood. "It'll be me next," he was telling her. "I can't run without Alfie, and if I can't race I can't win. And if I can't win, they'll take me away just like Alfie."

She cried, throwing her arms around him. "I won't let them take you, not ever. I promise you I won't. I promise." She rocked him gently, burying her face in his neck. "We'll stay together, you and me. No matter what. No matter what."

Becky wanted to stay out on the moor and ride as far as she could, for as long as the light lasted. Before she left High Moor she called out a goodbye to her father, as she always did. Where she rode that afternoon she did not know, and she did not care. She just rode. With Brighteyes beside her, she followed a tumbling stream from the pool on High Moor, along a rock-strewn track through a forest of stunted oak trees into a valley of scattered boulders and soggy marshland, until they came at last on to a narrow track with rushy fields on either side.

She could see in the distance now a ramshackle farmstead, a glowering place, where the mists hung over the fields, as if hiding some terrible secret. It looked deserted. She was in two minds as to whether she should go on or not, until she saw a chimney and smoke rising from it. Then from somewhere she heard a radio playing. Intrigued but still wary, she walked Red on past a field strewn with long abandoned farm machinery. Crows were perched there, dozens of them, and all were watching her silently as she passed.

Becky could see no one, but she sensed danger in this desolate place, and so did Brighteyes. His whole body tensed, his ears pricked. Then Becky saw the Land Rover parked outside the farmhouse, a battered grey Land Rover, just like the one that came to take away the dogs, that had taken Alfie away the day before. A gunshot rang out from beyond the farm buildings. Crows lifted off and scattered skywards, through the mists, cawing raucously. Red shied and reared, but somehow Becky managed to stay on. She dismounted, whispering to him, smoothing his nose, trying to settle him down again.

Brighteyes was growling from the back of his throat. He had seen the man before she had. The man was whistling as he came into view. He was pushing a wheelbarrow. He wore the same flat cap and the same dirty blue overalls. Becky could see quite clearly now what was in the wheelbarrow. A dead greyhound. Black and white. Alfie. It was Alfie. Becky's pulse was pounding in her ears. She stifled the scream rising inside her, as she watched him wheeling the barrow out into a nearby field. That was when Becky saw the mound of newly dug earth and a spade stuck into the top of it. Beyond this grave there were dozens of other mounds, some with the earth freshly turned, but most already grassed over.

A terrible grief and a fierce anger gripped Becky's heart as she looked out over this hateful killing field, as she watched Alfie being dumped into his grave. She turned and walked away weeping silently. She could feel Brighteyes beside

her, his face against her leg. One glance between them told her he had seen and understood everything. In the moments that followed Becky decided exactly what she had to do.

She took her time riding back over the darkening moor. She stopped off for a short while by her rock on High Moor, partly to postpone her return to the farmhouse for as long as she could, and partly to say goodbye to her father, to tell him what she was going to do. "I'll be back one day, Dad, I promise," she said as she left. "But I don't exactly know when."

Once back in the farmyard she led Red to his stable, fed him and said her last goodbyes. She took Brighteyes to his kennel and put out some food for him. "I won't be long," she whispered, getting up to go. "Then we'll be out of here, for good. I know you don't want it, but try to eat. You'll need it."

Craig and her mother were in the sitting room with the television on. To avoid them she went in

 119

the back door and up the back stairs to her bedroom, where she sat on her bed to write the letter she would be leaving behind. She kept it short.

Dear Mum,

I'm going away with Brighteyes. I don't know where, just away. I know it's not your fault, but you promised me Alfie was going to be looked after. That's what he told you. That's what he told me. I can't even write his name, I hate him so much. Sometimes I've even hated you, Mum, because you take his side, because you won't stand up to him enough, even when he rubbishes Dad, and because you won't leave him even though you know he's a monster, and I just can't understand that.

I want to tell you what I've just seen, but I can't write it because I'll remember it too well. Just tell him that I know what really happened to Alfie, and to all the *dogs when he sends them away, because I've seen it with my own eyes. And I'm not going to let it happen to Brighteyes. One day even Brighteyes will start losing, or he'll break down like Alfie and he'll be no use any more for racing. Then <u>he'll</u> do the same thing to Brighteyes as he did to all the others. So I'm taking him away before the Land Rover does. Don't worry about me. Brighteyes and I will look after one another.*

I love you Mum, but I just can't be around <u>him</u> any more.

Becky

She folded the letter and slipped it under her pillow. Later her mother called her down for supper. She went because she didn't want to arouse suspicion, and because she was hungry, and because she didn't know when she'd be eating again. She tried not to look at Craig at all, but their eyes did meet once, and she stared at him, telling him with that one withering look just how much she loathed and despised him. She hardly said a word to anyone all through the meal, and afterwards went upstairs just as soon as she could. When her mother came to say good night, she pretended to be asleep. Hidden away in the bottom of her cupboard was her rucksack already packed, and all the clothes she was going to wear later that night were ready under her bed.

It was a long wait. Becky needed to be quite sure they were both fast asleep before she made a move. When she got up at last, she trod lightly down the stairs. There was a blustery wind that night, that shook the house and rattled the doors and windows, so any sound she made was well camouflaged. She slipped silently out of the house. It was a clear, moonlit night. As she crossed the yard she began whispering to the dogs to let them know it was her. The last thing she wanted was for them to start barking. There was a whimper or two from them as she let Brighteyes out of his kennel, but nothing more. She put on his coat, and then, with Brighteyes close on her heels, she was running up the farm track and away. At the top of the hill she stopped for one last look at the farm below her. "I'm sorry, Mum," she breathed. Then she hitched up her rucksack, and set off down the road that would lead to wherever she was going. Where that would be she had no idea.

Up to this point her plan for their escape had been very specific in its detail. But now they were in unknown territory. All she knew was that she and Brighteyes were walking the road that led to the rest of the world, and they would follow wherever it went. Just so long as she didn't ever have to see Craig again, just so long as Brighteyes was with her and safe, she didn't mind.

For at least a couple of hours no car came by.

 123

The wind was chilling her to the bone, and up on the moor there was no shelter from it. She hadn't thought it would be this cold. She had her coat on and Brighteyes had his jacket on, but neither was enough to keep out the biting wind. And Becky had other worries too, that her mother might already have discovered she was gone, that Craig would be coming after them in the van. She knew she was going to have to hitch a lift, something her mother had always told her never to do. So when at last she saw headlights in the far distance, her first instinct was to duck down in the bracken at the side of the road and hide. But as the lights came closer, she could hear it wasn't a van, but a lorry of some kind. She felt confident enough then to run out and try to hitch a lift.

It turned out to be a cattle truck and the driver seemed friendly enough, even if he was a bit inquisitive. "Out late, aren't you?" he asked. Becky said she'd missed the last bus home, and she'd have to walk – the lie came easily.

He said he was on his way to a market "up country", to somewhere Becky had never heard of. She didn't know what "up country" really meant, but a ride to anywhere was a lot more inviting at that moment than freezing out on the moor. She could feel the warmth of the cab on her face, and "up country" sounded far enough away. They climbed in, Brighteyes curling up on the seat beside her, and at once making himself at home. The driver asked a few questions, but mostly about the dog, then fell silent and just drove on into the darkness, listening to the radio.

Cocooned in the stuffy heat of the cab both Becky and Brighteyes soon fell asleep. When Becky woke, it was early morning and they were pulling into a petrol station somewhere on the edge of a town. The driver looked across at her, as he turned off the engine. "Bit young to be out travelling on your own, aren't you?" he said.

"I'm eighteen," Becky said quickly, "and anyway I'm not on my own, am I? I've got the dog and he's got a bite." But she knew he was suspicious, that she hadn't convinced him, which is why, while he was paying for his petrol, she got out of the cab with Brighteyes and ran off.

There was a coach station in the centre of town and one coach waiting, engine running, to go.

Becky didn't care where to, as long as it was far enough away from Craig. She had some money with her, but not much – just £35.75, but that was more than enough to pay for the coach fare. She didn't like to spend the money – she knew she'd need it later – but she had no choice. If she tried hitching again there could be more questions, awkward questions. On a coach at least she'd be with lots of other people. There'd be safety in numbers, and besides mostly people didn't talk on coaches. That's what she thought. She was wrong.

As it was, she found herself, with Brighteyes beside her, sitting on the back seat next to the most talkative and inquisitive old lady on the planet, who immediately asked where she was going. Becky made up some complicated story about visiting her granny in the city and that her granny loved the dog like another grandchild, which was why they were going together. The more Becky elaborated and extended her story, the easier she found it. Luckily the old lady seemed to believe her. She clearly liked her too because she gave her some of her cheese sandwich, and some for Brighteyes too. Then for the next couple of hours, she rambled on about her own grandchildren who were scattered all over the world from Australia to South Africa. She showed her photographs of them and some of their letters too. And then at last, to Becky's great relief, she dropped off to sleep.

Becky had never liked cities, but as the coach crawled through the traffic, into the heat of the city, she knew it was the right place to be. Here they could lose themselves with no trouble at all. No one could ever find them. So when she walked out of the coach station with Brighteyes, into the streets, where everyone seemed to know where they were going and were in a tearing hurry to get there, it made her feel suddenly very bewildered and alone. She saw a bus going by. The sign on the front said Stanley Park. "We'll go to the park," she said to Brighteyes. "Then you can have a run." She didn't want to spend any more money on fares so she followed where the bus went, which was easy because the traffic was heavy and slow, and there always seemed to be another Stanley Park bus coming by which they could follow as well. It was a long walk, but the buses told Becky she'd get there sooner or later, so she just kept going.

When they did finally walk out on to the grass of Stanley Park, Brighteyes seemed to know at once that he could take off, and he did. Other dogs – there seemed to be mostly poodles in the park that day – raced after him, trying to keep up with him. They couldn't get near him, but that didn't stop them trying, again and again. He dodged and weaved, running circles round all of them. Becky sat on a bench loving every moment of it, glowing with pride. The sun was out now and warming her through. She felt suddenly happy. She knew then as she watched Brighteyes gambolling about that whatever happened, she had done the right thing, and that her father would think so too.

It was this unexpected surge of happiness that made her get up and race after him, made her forget her rucksack. When she came back with Brighteyes it was no longer there on the bench where she'd left it. All her spare clothes were gone, a blanket from her bed at home and all her photos of her mother and father, everything. All she had left was the money in one of her coat pockets, and a few biscuits for Brighteyes in the other. She sat down and cried then, mostly because she was so angry with herself. In that moment of despair, if she'd had her mobile with her, she'd most certainly have rung her mother right away, just given up and called the whole thing off. But she had left it at home deliberately, because she had known that sooner or later, she'd be bound to weaken.

Brighteyes stood there looking up at her, still panting after his run around. It was a knowing look, and one that Becky understood at once. "I know what you're saying," she said, wiping away her tears. "You're saying: no use sitting there feeling sorry for yourself. You're saying: I'm hungry." She gave him the last of the biscuits, then counted out the money she had left. "£8.32. Not much is it, Brighteyes? But we've got to eat. I'm hungry too." They shared a hot dog between them, had a long drink from a water fountain and set off across the park.

By evening the rest of her money was almost gone. Becky had bought a couple of apples, two bread rolls, some cheese and a blanket from a market stall, but all the while she was wondering how you go about finding a place to spend the

night in the city when you haven't got enough
money to pay for it.

As evening came on she was wandering the
streets still looking for a quiet place to shelter,
and this was when she discovered she wasn't the
only one out there on the streets with nowhere

to go. So many of the best places that were under cover and out of the wind – shop doorways, arcades, underpasses – were already occupied by the people of the street. Some were playing a flute or an accordion. Some were sitting there b e g g i n g and others were already asleep in sleeping bags or under cardboard

boxes. Many had dogs as well, who would bare their teeth and growl at Brighteyes as they passed by, or even lunge at him, snarling and snapping.

There were old men glaring at her with eyes like those of hungry, angry wolves, young men and girls no older than she was, lost in their sadness, looking but hardly seeing, their faces pale, their eyes sunken. There was one man standing on a corner begging. He was dressed in a kilt with bare legs and bare feet, banging away on a drum, chanting out his sad and angry mantra, "I'm homeless. I'm hopeless. You don't care, and I don't care. I'm homeless. I'm hopeless..."

She felt sorry for them, but was frightened of them too. More than once she was tempted to seek out the company of the younger ones, to try to share their bit of sheltered territory, but she was wary of approaching them. She knew instinctively that if she sat down with them she would sooner or later become one of them, become like them, and that was enough to keep her walking. Her legs ached, her feet ached. The wind was getting up all the time and with the darkness had come the cold. She had to find shelter, and soon.

She determined to keep clear of the street people, so she kept walking till she had left the lights and noise of the city centre behind her and found herself in quiet, tree-lined streets where there were small gardens at the front of the houses, and she could see lights on in the windows and people at home, people like her. These streets may have been darker, but she felt safer here somehow. There were just the two of them again now, so she could talk to Brighteyes freely. She knew he needed that, that he felt frightened and insecure in this strange world, just as she was.

"We'll find somewhere, Brighteyes," she told him. "Don't you worry, but it's got to be somewhere where there's no people, and no dogs either. We can have supper then. Bread and cheese. You don't like apples much, do you?" He padded along beside her, looking up at her

 135

whenever she spoke. "Better than being in that kennel, right? And better than being where Alfie is, that's for sure. We'll find somewhere. Soon, I promise." It helped Becky to talk, kept her spirits up when she needed it most, kept her hopes up when she felt at her most helpless.

After trudging along streets of terraced houses for an hour or so they came to a house which looked different from the others. There were no lights to be seen. Every window was boarded up. There was a builder's skip outside in the road. The place was obviously being renovated, so it had to be empty. Becky opened the little iron gate and peered into the front garden. An old garden shed stood in the corner behind the hedge, the door open and swinging in the wind. There was no one about. It was worth a risk, worth a look.

The shed turned out to be a perfect hideaway, small and snug with a pile of sacks in one corner that made a perfect bed. Becky pulled the door to

behind them, and they made it their own. They ate together, Becky sharing out the bread and the cheese. "One for you, one for me," was the only way to do it fairly. Brighteyes was so hungry he barely chewed at all before swallowing, and then he was waiting for the next offering. Becky was ravenous too, but even so she forced herself not to eat it all at once, but save a little for later: just half a bread roll and half an apple. Not much, but something. It would do for breakfast.

As she was feeding Brighteyes, she talked to him, but in a whisper. "No one'll find us here, not if we're careful. We can creep in here every night. No one'll know." The blanket she'd bought was just about big enough to cover them both. Lying there in the dark, the shed smelt musty and damp, and it creaked horribly in the wind. Sometimes she could hear footsteps going by outside, and voices too, but none of that mattered to Becky. She was asleep almost at once.

She slept fitfully but deeply, in and out of episodic dreams, and in every one of them her father was there. He was up on the rock on High Moor, pushing her on a swing, and she was shrieking out to him: "Higher! Higher! Higher!" He was coming out of the shop with the milk in his hand, and the lorry was hurtling down the hill, heading straight for him. As she slept and dreamed, Brighteyes lay there listening to her breathing, to the night noises of the city, all the while alert for danger, knowing it was out there somewhere, that he had to be ready for it, whatever it was.

Early the next morning, leaving the blanket behind in their hideaway, they stole out into the street and went down to the river. Geese came flying in, some ducks and a heron or two. Brighteyes sat watching it all intently, and didn't seem to want to come away when Becky called him. "We'll come back, Brighteyes," she told him. "I'm cold. I've got to keep walking, or I'll freeze."

So they walked on along the river until they came to a park with trees all around and ponds. There were swings here and slides, with children shouting and laughing and playing. For a while Brighteyes was happy just to watch them, his ears swivelling constantly as he listened. In the end he just couldn't resist it. He ran off to be with the children, bounding around them and barking playfully. Becky called him back, but it was too late. A couple of the children had taken fright and were running screaming to their mothers.

"He won't hurt," Becky told them. "Honest, he won't. He's really gentle."

But one of the mothers turned on her. "You keep him away!" she shouted. "You keep him under control, or I'll call the police."

"It should be on a lead anyway," said another of the mothers. "Should have a muzzle."

"He doesn't need a lead," Becky told them. "And he doesn't need a muzzle either. He was just having a bit of fun, that's all."

Then there were half a dozen angry mothers on their feet, yelling at her and Brighteyes, who stood there looking perplexed and upset. He turned and ran back to Becky. They left the park with abuse ringing in their ears.

It came on to rain later. So they went and sat in a bus shelter for a while, and that's where they finished the last of their food. Becky counted her money once again, hoping it was more than she knew it was, that somehow she'd made a mistake. She hadn't. It was still £1.56p. When a police car came by, slowing as it passed them, Becky kept her face hidden, pretending to be petting Brighteyes. They'd be on the lookout for her – she was sure of it. They'd have some kind of description of her by now: fifteen-year-old girl, green coat, jeans, woolly hat, with a light fawn greyhound with a tartan jacket. She might be able to hide her face but she couldn't hide Brighteyes. She thought the police car would be bound to stop, but it didn't. It was enough of a scare though to move Becky on, rain or no rain. The police car would be back to have another look any time, she was sure of it.

It took her a while to find the street again – she'd forgotten the name of it – and the house with the boarded-up windows and the skip outside. She'd decided that their garden shed home was the safest place to be for the moment, and the driest too.

One look from the end of the street, though, and her heart sank. The builders were there, two or three of them at least, carrying wood and bricks into the house. There was worse to come. As they walked by on the opposite pavement she saw that the skip looked much fuller than before. It took a moment or two for her to recognise what was in it – their garden shed, or what was left of it. She caught a glimpse of their blanket in amongst the wreckage of the shed. She was tempted to dart across the road to retrieve it, but the builders were constantly coming and going, and she didn't dare.

How far she wandered after that and where she went, Becky had no idea. She was lost now in a daze of misery and cold. At one point she went into a café and spent the last of her money on a mug of hot tea and a sticky bun. She gave half the sticky bun to Brighteyes who sat by her knee shivering and shaking uncontrollably. Becky made her tea last as long as she could. With nowhere else to go, staying in the warm was everything, and Becky knew that.

From where she was sitting by the window, she could see a phone box across the road. Just a few short steps, one call home, and she could be back there, tucked up in her warm bed. It would be so easy. But every time she was tempted she thought of Alfie: of Alfie and Brighteyes side by side, bounding over the moor; of Alfie alone in his kennel, carrying his hurt leg, limping towards her, the last time she'd seen him alive; then Alfie lying dead in that wheelbarrow. Use that phone, go back home and the same thing would happen to Brighteyes. She'd rather die first.

The lady behind the counter who had poured her tea had been watching her for a while now. Becky could feel it and had avoided looking at her, pretending instead to sip her tea which had long since been finished. But when she came over to her table Becky had to look up at her. She was about her mother's age, a black lady in a flowery apron. Becky expected to be kicked out, expected the woman to be angry. But she wasn't, not at all. "You want some more tea, girl?" she asked.

"Haven't got any money left," Becky replied.

"That's not what I asked now, is it? I said, you want some more tea?"

"Yes, please."

"And water for the dog?"

"Thanks."

She brought both, as well as a whole plate of bread and butter and jam. As she put it down on the table, she bent down and spoke to Becky softly, so none of the other customers could hear her. "You want some advice, girl? Whatever it is, I'm telling you it can't be that bad. You go home to your mum. She'll be worried sick about you.

You can't stay here for ever, and there's nothing out there 'cept streets, and they're not nice places for a young girl like you. You hear me? You be a good girl, and you go home now. And by the way, I got to say, that dog you got is the most beautiful dog I ever saw."

Becky wanted to tell her everything at that moment, the whole story, and maybe she would have too, had the lady not turned away to serve someone else at the counter. After that she always seemed to be busy making tea or washing-up. Becky eked out her tea and bread and jam as long as she could. Brighteyes loved the strawberry jam in particular, and went on licking his lips and enjoying it long after he'd swallowed it down.

She stayed on in the café until the lady behind the counter told her she'd really have to go because it was shutting-up time. "You're not going home, are you?" she said, as Becky went to the door. Becky shook her head. "I didn't think you were. You got to do what you got to do, am I right? But you got to keep yourself warm, girl. Try the library, about a mile down the road. Nice and warm in there."

So that's where Becky headed. It was warm all right, but they didn't allow dogs. It was the same with the museum. No dogs. She didn't even get through the front door there. She went and sat in a launderette for a while, but they kicked her out because she hadn't brought any washing to do. The waiting room at the bus station was empty and it was warm. She lay down on the bench with Brighteyes beside her and just hoped no one would come. She was half asleep when a bus inspector came in, and asked her which bus she was waiting for. She was too dozy to make up a credible story. She just couldn't think fast enough. So she told him the truth.

"I just wanted to stay in the warm," she said, "that's all. Got nowhere else to go."

"That's not my fault, is it?" he said, holding the door open. "Out, or I'll call the police."

Becky knew she had no choice, that it was no use arguing with a man like that. But all the same she took her time, very deliberately walking around the waiting room, looking at all the posters on the wall, studying the timetables and the maps, before sauntering past him without even an acknowledgment that he was there. She enjoyed her little show of defiance – it made her feel a little better about facing the dark, cold streets.

The rain had stopped by now, but the wind was icy. There seemed nowhere left to hide from it. All she could do was walk. It was already night before Becky came across the only refuge she could find, a disused multi-story car park with a high chain link fence all around, and a sign up outside: KEEP OUT. SECURITY PATROLLED She was desperate by now. She had to find some shelter, any shelter. So when she spotted a hole in the fence just about big enough to squeeze through, she didn't hesitate.

The place was filled with a hollow, eerie silence that frightened her, but it looked and sounded deserted. And most importantly it was dry and out of the wind. She found a tucked away corner down in the basement. Others had clearly discovered it before her. The place was littered with cardboard and plastic bags, and bottles, lots of bottles. Someone had lit a fire there too at one time or another, because there was a heap of ashes nearby. Brighteyes went to lie down at once on the cardboard and began cleaning himself. "That's what I like about you," Becky said. "Wherever you are, you just make the best of it, make yourself at home. But you're right: home is where you are, however horrible it is. So we'll make the best of it. Tomorrow I'll get some money, somehow. Then we can get a proper place and proper food." She went to sit down beside him, drew up her legs and hugged them to her. "I can do waitress work. Or kitchen work, washing-up and stuff like that. We'll go looking tomorrow. We'll be all right. We'll be fine, you'll see." She lay down then and pulled him close, her head against his chest. She felt the warmth of sleep coming over her and let herself drift with it.

It seemed to Becky that she was woken only minutes later. Brighteyes was on his feet and growling. Somewhere in the car park there was the sound of footsteps. Whoever it was, was coming closer. The light of a torch danced on the ceiling, then on the walls, then it was shining straight at her. Dazzled now, Becky put up her hands to protect her eyes.

"That's my place you're sleeping in. What the bleeding heck do you think you're doing here?"

The man's voice was rasping and angry, his words slurred with drink. Becky couldn't see his face. But suddenly out of the glare of the light came a dog, charging at her, his barking angry and loud, a terrifying war cry that echoed through the building. Before Becky could move, Brighteyes leaped at the dog, and then both were at each other yelping and snapping. Rough hands grabbed Becky and yanked her to her feet. "What've we got here then? A little girlie?" Becky could smell the stink of his breath. She kicked at him, and heard him cry out. Then she shook herself free of him and ran, calling for Brighteyes,

screaming for him. She could hear the two dogs still fighting somewhere ahead of her in the darkness, and ran towards them. She could see them now rolling on the ground, locked together in ferocious combat, snarling and tearing at one another.

Becky didn't hestitate. She rushed forward and tried to pull them apart. She managed to get hold of Brighteyes round his neck and drag him away. But the other dog came after her, and that was when she was bitten. She felt the teeth sink into her wrist and shake it, tugging at it, twisting it. She tried to break free, but the dog would not let her go. She could hear the man stumbling towards her, dropping his torch as he came, cursing loudly and roaring at her like a wild animal. Terrified, Becky lashed out at the dog, punching him hard on his nose again and again till he let her go. Suddenly free, she and Brighteyes ran for it, out of the basement, the whole car park resonating with angry shouting and barking. Then they were out in the open, back through the gap in the fence and away.

They kept running down the dark and empty street until Becky could run no more. Her head was swimming. Her wrist throbbed and her legs were so weak she could scarcely walk. She felt the blood dripping from her hand, knew that she'd been badly hurt, that she needed help; but all she could think of now was to keep going, to find somewhere to hide in case the man came after them.

Then she was aware of lights all about her. She found herself wandering aimlessly through a deserted shopping centre, which was where she came across some large recycling bins under an arcade. She was staggering by now, and knew her legs could not carry her much further. This was as good a place as any to hide. She crawled in behind the bins with Brighteyes and they huddled there silently, Becky rocking herself, trying to forget the agony in her wrist, trying to calm her panic. She could see now that Brighteyes too was wounded, that one of his ears was badly torn. She tried to reach out to him, but found she could not lift her arm. She tried to talk to him, and found her voice echoing strangely in her head. When she found herself lying on the ground, she couldn't work out how she'd got there, because she'd been sitting up a moment before. She tried to sit up again and couldn't find the strength. Brighteyes was swimming in and out of her vision. She tried to stop herself from fainting, but there was nothing she could do.

When the binmen came first thing the next morning, they discovered a girl lying semi-conscious behind the bins. She was bleeding badly. Standing over her was a fawn coloured greyhound who, from the look of him, had been in a nasty fight. They wouldn't have found her at all, they'd have driven off without ever seeing them, they told the paramedics, if the greyhound

hadn't come over and barked and barked at them, until they took some notice of him, and then he'd deliberately led them back to where she was. The paramedics told them that in that case, if the girl lived – and that was doubtful because she'd lost a lot of blood – it would be the greyhound who had saved her life.

*　　*　　*

I'm a running dog, a chasing dog, a racing dog. I'm not a fighting dog. I never in all my life had a fight before that night. My speed had always got me out of trouble before. This time I didn't have a chance to use it. He came at us out of nowhere, leaped straight at my face, teeth bared and snarling. He may have been small but he was all aggression, all muscles, all teeth, and I realised at once that he'd rip my throat out if he could. So I fought back with all my strength because I knew I was fighting for my life. It was him or me.

For a while I gave as good as I got, but I very soon understood that I was neither strong enough nor cunning enough. I was up against a street fighter, a killer dog. As we tussled and tore at each other, I could feel my strength ebbing fast. If Becky had not pulled us apart when she did, it would have ended much worse for me. As it was I got away with a bloodied ear. Becky was not so lucky.

I didn't really know how badly hurt she was until we were through the fence, and running through the streets, until I looked back and saw she was staggering rather than running. I stopped to wait for her. She was leaning against a lamp post now, so I ran back to her. "It keeps bleeding," she said. She was breathing hard and clutching her wrist. "It won't stop bleeding."

We walked on after that, Becky talking all the while, but after a time I realised she wasn't talking to me at all, but to herself. And she wasn't walking straight either. She kept bumping into me, kept stumbling off the pavement. Several times she ended up on her hands and knees, unwilling or unable to get up. I would try to encourage her to her feet again, and on we'd go, until at last we came into the glaring light of shop windows. She found a hiding place in behind some bins and crawled in, calling me after her.

She clung to me. "I'm so tired, Brighteyes," she whispered, "so tired." She was finding it difficult to talk at all now. She leaned her head back against the wall, closed her eyes and rested a while, before she opened them again. That was when she noticed my ear. "Oh, Brighteyes," she cried. "What have I done to you? We can't go on like this, can we? In the morning I'm going to take you to a rescue centre somewhere – I'll ask around – a proper one, not Craig's kind, and I'll leave you there. I don't want to do it, Brighteyes, you know I don't; but there's no other way. They'll look after you. They'll find you a good home. Then I'll ring Mum, and she'll come and fetch me. I may not see you again, but at least you'll be safe, won't you? And that's the main thing."

A moment later her eyes closed again and she slumped sideways to the ground. I tried waking her because I suddenly felt very alone without her voice to comfort me, but she was not sleeping as she usually slept. She was lying there unnaturally still, dead to the world it seemed, her face pale, paler than I'd ever seen it, white almost. I curled up beside her, my head resting on her shoulder. She needed to be warm, I thought, and so did I. But both of us were so cold by now that between us we had no warmth to share.

I was woken by the rumbling of a lorry nearby, and the sound of men's voices. There was the clatter and crash of breaking bottles. They were emptying the bins. To begin with I stayed hidden where I was. Becky had not woken. I could not understand why not. With all the noise of the lorry and the binmen so close by, their voices so loud, I knew something was very wrong. Nothing I did made any difference. She would not wake.

I ran out from behind the bins, barking at them. They seemed taken aback at first, frightened almost, which wasn't what I intended at all. I stood there, barking for a while, then ran back behind the bins and out again, trying to make them come and see, trying to make them understand. It was a while before they did, before one of them approached me. He was quite wary of me. He crouched down and reached out to pat me. "What's your problem, son?" he asked, stroking my neck now. "Nasty looking ear. You've been in a bit of a punch-up, haven't you?"

This time when I ran off behind the bins, he followed me to where Becky was lying. "Jeez!" he shouted. "Call the ambulance! Call 999 fast! There's a girl back here, and she's hurt bad! Quick!"

I stayed with Becky until they came and took her away. I tried to jump up into the ambulance with her, but they wouldn't let me. "No dogs in the ambulance I'm afraid. Not allowed. Hygiene rules," said the lady who'd been looking after Becky.

"He saved the girl's life," said the binman. "You said so yourself. You could make an exception, couldn't you? Where's he going to go?"

"Sorry," she said, getting into the ambulance. "I suggest you take him to the police station down Willoughby Road. They'll look after him."

The binmen tried to hold on to me but I wouldn't have it. I broke free and took off after the ambulance as it raced away down the road, lights flashing, sirens blaring. Sometimes it almost got away from me, but whenever it ran into traffic and had to slow down, I'd catch up with it. Dodging the cars or the people on the pavements, I just about managed to keep it in sight.

I had lost Patrick, my first best friend. I had been stolen away from him and would never see him again. I had lost Alfie, who'd been like a father and brother to me. I did not want to lose Becky, who was doing all she could to save my life. So I ran after the ambulance, as if Alfie was at my side. There was no way I was going to let that ambulance get away. When it turned off the road I followed it down the driveway. When they carried Becky into the hospital I tried to go in after her, but they wouldn't let me past. They shouted at me and waved me away. So I went and sat on the grassy bank below the car park, and waited. Becky had gone in. Sooner or later she would have to come out again. I would wait for her. She had not deserted me. I would not desert her. Besides, I had nowhere else to go.

All day I had a lot of attention from passers-by, and

some of it came with gifts of chocolate or biscuits or crisps, all of which I accepted gratefully and quickly snaffled up. Children came and sat beside me for a while, patted me and talked to me. I liked that. But all the while I didn't take my eyes off the entrance to the hospital, watching everyone come and go, looking all the time for Becky, waiting for her to come out. She had gone in, so she had to come out. I would stay until she did.

As dark came down there were fewer and fewer people about, and no children at all. I missed them. Ambulances came and went. I did see the lady who'd carried Becky into the ambulance, the one who hadn't let me go with her. She didn't see me though. She was too busy driving her ambulance. I tried again and again to sneak in through the door and find Becky, but I got chased out every time. I was getting tired, and I was so, so cold. I felt like going off and finding myself

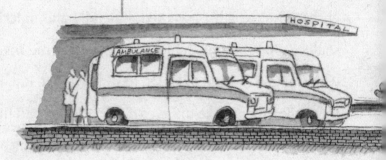

somewhere to shelter out of the wind, somewhere I could curl myself up tight and sleep. But I knew I mustn't. I knew Becky could come out at any moment. I had to stay where I was and stay awake.

I'm not sure which came first, the thought that I was hungry or the smell of food. Suddenly I found there was an old man sitting down beside me. He didn't smell like anyone else I had ever met. In fact he didn't smell like a man at all. He just smelled of food, and it was the kind of food I liked a lot. He put something down in front of me on the grass. "Baked

tatty, with my best cheese filling," he said. "I thought
you could do with it, warm you up. You're shaking like
a leaf. Go on, help yourself." I was hungry all right, but
I still hesitated. "Oh I see," the old man went on, "so

you're the shy sort, just like Paddywack. He'd never eat with anyone looking either. I won't look, promise."

The potato was full of melted cheese. It was delicious and gone all too soon. I licked the grass until there was no trace of it left.

"Glad you liked it," he said. "You've made quite a stir round here. Everyone's been talking about you all day. Lynn told me about you when she came for her tatty at lunchtime – one of my best customers she is. She told me how you followed her ambulance with that girl in it all the way here, going like the clappers she said. Turbo-charged. But I've been watching you. You've been sitting right here all day long, haven't you? You've been waiting for that girl to come out. Lynn told me her name. But I forget. I forget a lot these days, specially names. She won't be out for a while you know. Lost a lot of blood apparently. But she'll be all right, don't you worry. Lynn says she's a real survivor that one. Like you, I reckon. But you can't sit out here all night. Big frost tonight, minus four they said on the radio. There's no point you sitting here. They won't let her out now, not at night-time. They'll keep her in for another day or two at least, I should think."

That was when he leaned towards me, peering at me more closely. "Nasty ear you've got. It needs cleaning up. Here, I've got an idea. Why don't you come and sleep in my tatty van? You'll be snug as a bug in a rug. Baking it is in there. Well it would be, wouldn't it? It's what it's for, the Tattyvan. You don't know what I'm talking about, do you? I've got this old van. Looks like a sort of travelling potato, a motorised tuber, you might say. I converted it myself. My Tattyvan I call it, and I'm Mr Tattyvan when I'm out on the road. I'm Joe really, to my friends I mean.

"I go all over the place, baking potatoes and selling them – cheese filling, chilli, coleslaw, tuna mayo – take

 167

your pick, I make it all myself. The hospital here is one of my best pitches. Paramedics like Lynn, doctors, nurses, ancillary workers, visitors, patients, they all love my tatties. Well they would, wouldn't they? It's good healthy food, and cheap too. But tomorrow's my last day. Time has come for something different."

He pulled his bobble hat down over his ears and hugged himself. "I'm fruzzed sitting here." He got to his feet. "Are you coming then?" He was whistling for me as he walked away. Then he turned round and saw I wasn't moving. "So you're going to stay there and wait for her, are you? Loyal, faithful. I like that in a dog. I like that in people too. Just like poor old Paddywack. You've got a lot in common you two." And then he was gone away into the darkness.

I felt suddenly very alone. I liked the gentleness of his voice and his quiet kindliness. I thought I'd seen the last of him but he was back in a few minutes and this time he was carrying a blanket. "Here," he said, wrapping it around me. "This'll keep you a little warmer. I'll be back in the morning. See you then." And he was gone again.

It was a long and lonely night, and the coldest of my life, only interrupted by the occasional wailing siren as another ambulance drove up. I never fell asleep, not once, because the cold didn't let me. I kept watch on that door, hoping all the while that Becky would come out, but she didn't.

By first light Joe was back again and I was so pleased to see him. He brought me a bowl of warm milk, and I lapped it eagerly, filling myself with its warmth. He sat down beside me and rubbed me with his bobble hat until I wasn't shivering and shaking any more. And he talked to me the whole time.

"What am I going to do with you?" he was saying. "I mean, you can't sit out here for ever, can you?

I could take you down to the rescue centre, I suppose. That ear of yours needs seeing to." He tried to reach out and touch it, but I wouldn't let him. "They'd clean it up. They'd look after you, that's for sure, find you a good home. But you want to stay, don't you? You want to wait for her."

He was still sitting there, still talking, still rubbing me, when I looked up and saw someone I recognised walking towards us. It wasn't Becky. It was her mother.

"So there you are," she said to me. "They told me in the hospital I'd find you out here. I see you've found yourself a friend then."

Joe had got to his feet by now. "Yours is he?" he asked.

"He's Becky's really, my daughter's. They ran off together, the two of them. They had good reason, believe me. She had an accident, but she's all right now, thank God. Much better."

"That's good," Joe said. "So you'll be taking him home then, I suppose?"

"I don't think so," she replied. "We've got nowhere to keep him, not any more. As soon as she's out of hospital – probably tomorrow, the doctor says – we'll be moving on. Things didn't work out back home, so Becky and me, we'll be staying in my mum's flat for a while, just till we find somewhere on our own. We're better off on our own. Becky was right about that. She was right about a lot of things. But that's another story. Anyway, the trouble is, Mum's got cats, three of them. She loves them to bits, and she hates all dogs. So do the cats.

"I've talked to Becky about it. She's upset, of course she is. She'd love to keep him if she could, but she knows we can't. She'll be happy enough if she knows he's gone to a good home. It looks to me like maybe he's found one already."

171

For a few moments Joe didn't seem to know quite what to say. "To tell you the honest truth, I really hadn't thought about keeping him," he said. "It hadn't even occurred to me. I mean, I'm planning on being on the move a lot, I've got things to do, and I hadn't bargained on... But then maybe... maybe it'd be good to have a companion along, someone to talk to. He's a good listener, I know that." He smoothed my face and fondled my ears gently. "He's got kind eyes, just like Paddywack. My wife had a dog a bit like this. Paddywack, he was called, because she liked the song – y'know the one, 'Knick Knack Paddywack, give a dog a bone', that one. He was a lurcher, fast like a greyhound, faithful too. A good friend. Marion loved him, more than she loved me sometimes, I reckon. Yes, maybe it's a good idea at that."

"Well, old son," he went on, patting my neck gently, and looking me in the eye. "Haven't got much to offer you, except friendship. I've got lots of that." He smiled and I knew right away I was in safe hands, that here was someone I could trust. He looked up at Becky's mother, "All right, why not? If he'll have me, I'll have him. You tell that daughter of yours in the hospital not to worry, that he'll be well looked after, I promise."

"I'll tell her," said Becky's mother. She was crouching down over me now, her eyes full of tears. "I still don't understand it. How could he? They're so beautiful, so trusting. How could he have done it?"

"Done what?" Joe asked.

"Nothing," she said, standing up abruptly and moving away. "It's nothing. Anyway, he won't be doing it again – I made sure of that." She looked at me. "You'll give him a good life, won't you? He deserves it." And then she was gone, hurrying away from us back into the hospital.

"Botheration," said Joe after a while. "I never asked

 173

her what you were called, did I? Never mind. New life. New name. As it should be. I think I'm going to call you Paddywack. Marion would like that."

I had a place to sleep, on a blanket right by the baking oven in Joe's Tattyvan. I loved the warmth of the place and the smell of it and the cheese fillings too. I missed Becky, of course I did, just like I missed Patrick before her. I didn't forget them, they were a part of my life, a part of me. I knew how much they had loved me, how much I loved them and owed them. But now I was with Joe, and I knew we'd get on fine, that like Patrick and Becky, he was someone who would look after me, someone I could trust completely.

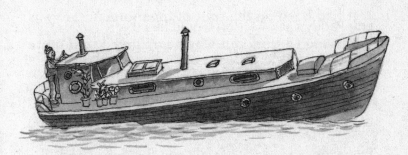

"Knick Knack, Paddywack"

Joe Mahoney didn't live in a house, not any more. He lived in a barge, on the canal. He'd been living there for nearly two years, and in all that time he'd lived there alone. This was the first time he'd ever invited anyone else on board. In fact, one way or another, Joe had been living alone for very much longer than that. He'd got accustomed to being on his own, and was wondering, as he drove home in the Tattyvan with Paddywack sitting beside him looking out of the window, whether he'd really done the right thing in taking him on.

It had been on the spur of the moment. He was still trying to work out why he'd agreed to it quite so easily, quite so quickly. Maybe it had been meant, he thought, fated in some way. After all, this was his last day on the road with the Tattyvan, the end of an era for him, and the beginning of another. There was something else though. The dog had a familiar look about him, almost as if old Paddywack had come back from the grave – not a lurcher maybe, but a greyhound was close enough. He had the same gentle look in his eye. And perhaps in the back of his mind was the thought that for what he was going to have to do, it would be good not to be alone. He hadn't been looking forward to the days that lay ahead, not one bit. It was just something that had to be done. Now at least he'd have someone to talk to, someone to be with.

Joe looked at him sideways and the dog looked back at him, as if waiting for him to say something. So he did say something. "Normally," Joe began, "normally I talk to myself, and not because I'm mad, not much anyway. It's because I like the sound of a voice, any voice. It's silences I don't like. Marion and me, we used to chat away all the time, and I miss that. I like the radio, like the sound of the water lapping around the barge, the ducks and the Canada geese – bit too noisy sometimes, they are, especially first thing in the morning. I expect you'd like to talk if you could, wouldn't you? But since you can't, I'll have to do the talking for the both of us, won't I?" The dog was licking his lips and panting. He seemed to be smiling, and he seemed to be listening too.

"I know what you're thinking, Paddywack. You're thinking: 'Who is this funny old bloke driving around in a van that looks like a giant potato.' You don't know the first thing about me, do you? So here it comes: potted history of Joe Mahoney, otherwise known as the Tattyman. Age sixty-nine. Car mechanic, learned it in the army, fixing Land Rovers, lorries, that sort of thing. Mr Fixit, Marion used to call me – she called me a lot of other stuff too, come to think of it." He chuckled then.

"I had this shed out at the back of the house, my workshop, and she'd ring the bell when it was time for tea. Sometimes I wouldn't hear it because I was always sawing or planing or drilling. Then I'd come in a bit late, and we'd have a right old row. But we fixed that too. 'Never let the sun go down on a quarrel,' she'd say, and we never did. She'd get mad at me because the tea was cold. Could she get mad at me!"

His laughter turned suddenly to tears. "Don't take any notice. I've done quite a bit of crying over the past few years, I can't seem to stop myself. Silly old fool I am. Well, she went and got ill, didn't she? Parkinson's disease it was. Not much at first – her head shook a little that's all. But then later when it got bad, she needed a lot of looking after. That's when I had to give up the regular job in the garage, and bought the Tattyvan – so I could be my own boss. I'd only go out in the Tattyvan when she was well enough to leave. Things worked out fine too, for a while. But then she got worse and she could see I wasn't coping any more. I said it was fine, but she wouldn't listen. She insisted. She said she'd go into Fairlawns, the nursing home down the road, and we had a bit of a row about that too. But she talked me round, like she always did.

"Anyway, Fairlawns turned out to be the best place in the world for her. Mrs Bellamy runs it like a ship, but she's a good and kind captain. Lovely caring people up there. Nothing was ever too much trouble. The trouble was, the Tattyvan wasn't bringing in enough money – I just wasn't out on the road often enough. That was part of the problem anyway. Couldn't pay the bills. Clever with engines, hopeless with money, that's me.

"So with money running short, I had to sell the house – I didn't like being there without Marion anyway. And that's when I bought the barge, bought it for a song. Never told her. There was no point. Her memory had gone – sometimes she didn't even know who I was. It was a funny thing; she talked a lot about Paddywack, asked about him a lot, asked why I never brought him in to see her – and he'd been dead for years, five or six years at least by this time. But he stayed alive in her head right to the end. Maybe she was right after all, maybe old Paddywack didn't die. He was just resting and now he's come back as you, if you see what I'm saying. She'd like that. She'd like you."

Joe parked the van in its usual place under the trees down by the canal, and let Paddywack out. He locked the van, and then patted it affectionately. "Been good to me, this old thing. 'My brilliant idea', I called it. Marion said I was mad, 'off my trolley', she said, I remember. But she had to laugh when she saw it."

The van was an old Bedford camper van, about forty years old. Joe had bought it for £150, restored it and done it up as his Tattyvan. He'd found an old Victorian oven in the same scrap yard where he'd discovered the van, and installed it in the back, built a serving counter with an opening hatch at one side and a little kitchen along the other, with a new sink and worktop too, and room for the gas cylinder underneath. But the best thing about it wasn't the ingenious potato baking technology, but the van itself. Joe had transformed it into one huge baked potato on wheels, with its own headlights and wipers, with its own chimney. He'd made and painted his own sign: "Mr Tattyman, Best baked potatoes in the whole world. Choice of fillings, £3 each." He'd hook it up on the side of the van whenever he found a pitch, on industrial estates, outside shopping centres and schools, at fêtes and carnivals, but most often outside the hospital because it wasn't too far from Fairlawns Nursing Home.

It was Marion who had first named it the Tattyvan, and named him Mr Tattyman too. After Marion first went into Fairlawns the business had gone quite well, for a while. Joe could be out in his Tattyvan for most of the day. It had novelty appeal, fun appeal. But the truth was there were never enough customers to make it pay, and Joe didn't like to put up the price of the potatoes because he thought the children wouldn't be able to afford them if he did – it was children outside school gates who made up at least half his customers.

But Joe didn't do it just for the money. He loved getting in his van every morning, being out there on the road; loved serving his regular customers who, like Lynn at the hospital, very soon became his friends. One of his favourite pitches had been the Fairlawns Nursing Home itself. His visits proved to be the highlight of the day for the old people. Every time he came to see Marion, several of them would come out and buy one of his potatoes. Then he'd go up and sit with Marion for a while afterwards before going home to his barge.

The barge had been a complete wreck when he'd bought it, rotting and rusting away and quite unable to move from its mooring. Joe had renovated it throughout and rebuilt the engine. And now, at long last, it was finished.

"There it is, Paddywack," he said proudly. "Your new home. What d'you think? I've called her *The Lady Marion* – seemed the right name. I started up the engine for the first time last week, and it works too, works a treat. Soon as I've done what I've got to do, done what I promised her, I'm going to move the potato oven from the van into the barge. We'll sell the Tattyvan, and then off we go, free as the birds. That's how we're going to live. We're going to chunter about all over the country, up and down the canals, tie up whenever we feel like it, wherever we want, and sell our potatoes to keep the pennies coming in. We won't get rich, but we'll do all right. I've worked it all out." He bent down and stroked Paddywack. "Till an hour or two ago I was going to do this alone. Some things just happen along. You just happened along, and I'm very glad you did. Come on board, old son, and I'll show you round."

Paddywack soon curled up on the chair by the wood-burning stove and looked about him.

The welcome smell of cooking was filling the barge. He lifted his nose and savoured it. "It's bacon," said Joe, laughing. "I hope you like it, because I eat an awful lot of it. You can have some of my rinds too. I've made them nice and crispy.

It's going to be a very long day tomorrow. From now on until it's over, every day's going to be very busy, and very long too, and the nights even longer still, I expect. You'll be wondering what I'm going on about, won't you. Since you'll be with me, I reckon you've got a perfect right to know. Come and get your bacon first. I've got digestive biscuits too. It's what I live on, bacon butties and brown sauce and digestive biscuits. But no potatoes. Never touch baked potatoes. Now there's a secret never to be told. Mr Tattyman hates his baked potatoes!"

Joe told him then all there was to tell about the promise he'd made to Marion. It had been one of the very last times Marion had recognised him. Joe was reading aloud to her, *Gone with the Wind*, her favourite book, when she interrupted, looking him straight in the eye. "Don't you let them do it, Joe," she whispered. "Promise you won't let them do it. Promise."

"I'll do what I can," Joe had told her, but that wasn't good enough.

She became quite agitated. "No, they mustn't close it. Miss Carter, my friends, what would happen to all my friends? You must promise." So he had, and there was no going back on it now.

Of course everyone at Fairlawns had talked about little else for months, ever since the article first appeared in the local newspaper. Many of the old people had become very anxious and upset. Miss Carter, the oldest of them at ninety-six and wheelchair bound, was usually full of the joys of life. But she had hardly spoken a word since the threatened closure was announced. She simply sat, staring into space, lost in deep sadness.

The Council was closing the nursing home down because it was too small – only a dozen beds – and the building was too old and dilapidated. It just wasn't "cost effective". That it was a much loved home to twelve old people, a place where they belonged, where they were wonderfully cared for, and where all their friends were, appeared to be of little concern to the Council. Fairlawns would close and everyone would be dispersed to other nursing homes, if others could be found, or if not, then to hospital. There had been thousands of letters of protest sent to the Council, and even to the Prime Minister. Deidre Besant, their member of Parliament, had pleaded to have Fairlawns kept open, in the House of Commons, on television and radio. She had done her best. Relatives, Joe among them, had picketed local councillors. Doctors and nurses were unanimous in their support: to close a nursing home, that was so well run, and when the need for such places was growing all the time, would be a disaster, they said. Newspaper reporters and photographers had been in and out of Fairlawns for months, interviewing staff and patients. The whole community was against closing it down. Yet nothing and no one seemed to be able to prevent it from happening.

Joe handed Paddywack the last of the digestive biscuits. "I had my promise to keep," he went on. "So if there was a protest, I was there. I organised the support group, collected signatures. Almost everyone who bought a potato off the Tattyvan signed the petition. I got over 15,000 signatures. Towards the end, when Marion was drifting in and out of consciousness, I'd tell her how well it was all going, how many more signatures we'd got, how the Council would have to listen now. I really hope she heard me, but if I'm honest with myself, I'm not sure she did. Sometimes I think it was a good thing she died when she did, because nothing came of any of it. A week after she died the Council announced the date they were closing Fairlawns down. And that's when I really got angry, when I decided to do it, to pack up the

Tattyvan for good and to make one last effort, to protest full-time, until they changed their minds. And by now it wasn't just because of the promise. Like I said, I was angry. That place, those people, they kept Marion happy. The old people were like brothers and sisters to her, like a family, Miss Carter in particular. And the staff did all they could for her, I reckon I owed them. So I've got my tent, my sleeping bag, my little stove, and tomorrow is the big day, the day it all begins."

He emptied the biscuit crumbs into his cupped hand, and let Paddywack lick them off. "Don't you worry, old son, we'll have plenty of biscuits in the tent, and plenty of bacon butties too. I want to be out there at Fairlawns by first light tomorrow morning. We'll pitch our tent, put up our banner and stay there for as long as it takes."

The next morning, drivers on their way to work in town saw a bright orange tent pitched on the wide grass verge by the road in front of the

Fairlawns Nursing Home. Beside it sat an old man in a tatty-looking duffle coat and a blue and white striped bobble hat, and right next to him stood a greyhound almost the same golden colour as the leaves on the tree above them. Behind them and above them, strung out between the branches hung a huge banner. Painted across it in multi-coloured letters was: SITTING HERE TILL FAIRLAWNS IS SAVED! HOOT TO SAVE FAIRLAWNS!

Hardly a driver passed by without hooting that morning. It was a great and hopeful start, and it got better. By lunchtime every single one of the old people from Fairlawns had made their way down the drive at one time or another, to the grass verge to see them, even Miss Carter in her motorised wheelchair. Suddenly she seemed to be her old self again. It was a sunny autumn day, a bit blustery with leaves flying, but still warm enough for each of them to stay there with Joe and Paddywack for a few minutes. They'd wave in

delight as the cars and lorries drove by, hooting
and honking their support. The matron, Mrs
Bellamy, was there most of the time, making sure
that none of the old people stayed out there too
long or got too cold. It was Mrs Bellamy's idea to
invite Paddywack back into the house.

"Look at him, Joe, he's shivering from head to tail," she said. "We'll have him inside for a while and get him out of this wind."

Paddywack found himself being led up to the house and into the warmth of the sitting room where he at once became the centre of attention.

He lay down in front of the fire and toasted himself, until all his shivers were gone. Whenever the old people called him over he would go and stand there beside them, and be stroked and adored for a while. For food he simply followed his nose to the kitchen and waited there until someone noticed him and fed him, which sooner or later they always did. And sometimes, when he heard the front door open, he'd nip out and trot down the drive to be with Joe again. He'd sit down right against Joe's leg, resting his head on his knee. He could doze easily that way, and as Joe already knew, Paddywack loved dozing even more than eating.

So for the next few days Paddywack was in and out of Fairlawns all day long, a pure delight for the old people to whom he was a new and welcome distraction, and a great source of joy. And what they loved best of all was to see him running, on the great wide lawn under the tree of heaven. Mrs Bellamy would throw sticks for Paddywack to chase after and retrieve, and sometimes Paddywack's sheer zest for running would take over and he'd forget the stick and go off on several laps of honour, racing round and round the tree of heaven, faster and faster, scattering fallen leaves. All the old people watching from the sitting room window would burst into applause. He made them feel young again, feel hopeful again. And for Joe, even as cold and tiredness set in, Paddywack was becoming the best of companions, a true and trusted friend. They'd spend the nights huddled together in the tent, keeping each other warm as best they could.

To begin with, the weather was kind to them, but then the rain came, and with it the first real cold of the winter. The tent gave them some protection from the wind and the rain, but Joe couldn't hide away in it for too long. To make the protest effective he knew he had to be out there where he could be seen. He had to be waving back at his supporters as they passed by. There were days when the weather was really foul, when Joe knew the cold and the wet were just too much for Paddywack. Then he would ask Mrs Bellamy if Paddywack could spend most of the day inside Fairlawns. But despite the warmth of the fire, and all the adoring attention of the old people, Paddywack would escape whenever he could and run down to the grass verge to be with Joe again. Joe loved him for that. The two would snuggle together under Joe's waterproof cape, with just their faces showing.

To pass the time Joe counted the number of

cars and lorries, and bicycles too, that hooted and honked and tinkled as they passed. Counting lifted his spirits, because more and more of them were doing just that. Support was growing. Every day, whatever the weather, more passers-by stopped to talk and pet Paddywack, and every day more journalists or radio interviewers or television crews would come by. And through it all Mrs Bellamy saw to it that Joe and Paddywack were well supplied with food from the kitchen in Fairlawns, so that Joe only had to use his stove for brewing up hot, sweet tea, which he did on the hour, every hour. That routine helped, because it was something to look forward to, something to warm him through, and he needed that badly. However hard he tried, Joe found it difficult to keep warm. The more the cold crept into his bones, the more he began to feel it was hopeless, despite all the support and attention the protest was getting. At times he would have given way completely to despair, had not Paddywack been there beside him, had not the old people kept coming down to be with them.

Despite all Mrs Bellamy's best efforts to keep them inside, there would always be one of the old people from Fairlawns to keep Joe company through his vigil, to wave back at the cars and to talk to the press. There was a rota now, which they kept to diligently. Each one would stay for about half an hour, and then be replaced by another, no matter how hard the icy wind blew. It became a point of honour now for them never to let Joe and Paddywack be alone out there. This was all Miss Carter's idea, which is why Mrs Bellamy had to go along with it, despite all her concerns for the health of the old people. No one argued with Miss Carter – Miss Carter had been a headmistress for forty years. But the truth was of course that Mrs Bellamy didn't want to argue with any of them. She felt too much solidarity with them, too much admiration for them. She was simply worried for their health. She made absolutely sure there was always one of the staff with them, and that they were always swathed in blankets and clutching hot water bottles.

A week went by and it was clear by now that two or three of the old people were suffering. Bob Larkin in particular was so weak one morning after a night of coughing that he could scarcely get out of bed. When Doctor Morrison was called to see him, he said that he had a chest infection, and must on no account go outside. He also insisted that Mrs Bellamy had to put a stop to all this before someone caught pneumonia. When Mrs Bellamy said she was powerless to do anything about it, Doctor Morrison called all the old people together in the sitting room. He gave them a severe lecture. "I respect what you are trying to do," he said as he finished. "I admire your courage and your determination. But this

 199

has gone far enough. We've already got Mr Larkin sick upstairs. You go out there in this weather and you're risking your lives. I can't be held responsible if you go on like this."

Miss Carter lifted her head slowly. "Maybe," she said in a steely voice. "Maybe. But they're our lives to risk, Doctor, aren't they?"

Mrs Bellamy tried again to persuade them once the doctor had gone, but it was no use. She went outside after that and sat with Joe and Paddywack by the tent. "It's you they're rallying around, Joe," she said. "You and Paddywack. I know you're doing it for Marion. But she wouldn't want this, I know she wouldn't. She'd say what I'm saying, that you should call it a day. You've done all you could, Joe. No one could have done more."

"Believe you me, Mrs Bellamy," Joe replied, "there's nothing I'd like better than to get back to my snug little barge and be warm again. It's a long time since I've felt my feet. And I'll be honest with you – there's been plenty of times when I've felt like giving up. But it's like Marion used to say: 'You're an obstinate old goat, Joe.' I am too. I started this thing, Mrs Bellamy, and I'm going to finish it. Sitting out here with Paddywack, I've had a lot of time to think things over, and the more I think, the angrier I get. They've got no right to close you down, to ruin the lives of everyone up at Fairlawns, and I won't let them. It's a matter of principle, as I see it. We've got to look after our old people. They've earned it. They deserve it. So, unless the old people themselves tell me to stop, me and Paddywack we'll sit this out. We'll stay here till we make the Council change their minds. That's all there is to it."

Mrs Bellamy knew there was no point in arguing any more, that Joe had quite made up his mind. "All right," she said, "but from now on, you

will spend your nights inside, in the warm. I can't sleep thinking of you out here all night. The cold air out here can't be good for you, nor for Paddywack. No arguments now."

So that's how it was arranged. Each night, Joe and Paddywack would pack up the tent, take down the banner and walk up the drive to Fairlawns. They had a spare room there, often used for visiting relatives – Joe had slept in it once or twice before, when Marion had been very poorly. A warm bath and a warm bed each night revived Joe's strength, and his spirits too. He would fall asleep almost at once, Paddywack stretched out beside him. Every night Joe felt so tired that he wanted to sleep for ever. When he woke each morning he would lie there for a while dreading the thought of another long day of cold ahead of him. But Paddywack would be standing by the door, waiting for him, tail wagging. Joe knew well enough what Paddywack was telling him. "Up you get, lazybones. We've got to be out there." So he'd drag himself out of bed and do what he was told. He'd pull on his clothes, get out there, pitch the tent, put up the banner, and settle down for another day of waving at supporters, of brewing tea, of counting cars.

But every day seemed an eternity now to Joe, colder and more uncomfortable than the one before. It was becoming clearer with every passing hour that not so many cars were hooting now, that the novelty of the protest was wearing thin. He began to lose heart. He was looking grey and drawn. Mrs Bellamy was worried about him. She brought Doctor Morrison down to see him. The doctor did his very best to persuade Joe to call a halt to the whole thing. No one was paying attention any more, he told him. There was just no point in going on.

It was while the doctor was down there with him that Paddywack suddenly stood up and trotted away up the drive, his tail wagging. Then Joe saw what Paddywack had seen. Miss Carter was coming down the drive in her motorised wheelchair. She was not alone. Mrs Bellamy counted them, they were all there, every one of them – even Bob Larkin who had got up from his sickbed. Out of Fairlawns they came, some walking arms linked, some on Zimmer frames, others in wheelchairs pushed by staff, a slow procession making its way down towards them. Paddywack was gambolling among them, barking with excitement.

"What's going on, Miss Carter?" Mrs Bellamy demanded.

"We've been talking," Miss Carter replied, "and we have all of us decided that from now on our place is down here alongside Joe and Paddywack. After all, Joe and Paddywack are doing this for us, for all of us at Fairlawns, and we can't just pop out for a few minutes to be with them. We have to be here like he is, all the time. We can't play at this any longer. And do you know who gave us this idea? It was Paddywack. He used to come inside with us, in the warm where he liked it, where we like it too. But then he stopped coming, didn't he? He decided that he had to be out here with Joe, whatever the weather. Well, so have we. What we'd like to ask you to do, Mrs Bellamy, if you wouldn't mind, is to bring out those wicker chairs from the conservatory for us, and maybe a cushion or two, and lots of blankets. We'll be fine." Mrs Bellamy was bursting to protest. "It's no use," Miss Carter went on. "We took a vote, didn't we? It was unanimous. We're going to come out here and sit with Joe and Paddywack, all day and every day, for as long as it takes, until the Council change their minds."

"You can't!" cried the doctor.

"We most certainly can, Doctor," Miss Carter told him. "And we will too, you just watch us. Are you with us, Mrs Bellamy?"

Mrs Bellamy was in tears by now. It was several moments before she regained her composure. "Well, Doctor," she said, wiping her eyes. "I don't think they've left us much choice, have they? So I suppose we're just going to have to make the best of it. I suggest you warn the hospital and the emergency services what's happening here. They'll need to know, just in case." She turned to Miss Carter then. "And, to answer your question, I am with you, of course I am. I always have been, you know that. We'll make you all as comfortable as we can, chairs and blankets like you said, but we'll need heaters and music too. Warm and happy. That's what we've got to be. Warm and happy. We'll play all the old songs, from the Beatles to Vera Lynn, all the ones you like, and we can sing along, can't we? That'll keep us happy."

Miss Carter drove her chair over to where Joe and Paddywack were sitting, swathed in blankets outside the tent. "You don't mind if we join you, do you?" she said.

"You're mad, Miss Carter, all of you are. Mad and wonderful." He reached out and took her hand. "You'll catch your death out here, you know that?"

"Outside, inside. What's the difference?" Miss Carter replied.

Things happened very quickly after that. Mrs Bellamy rang up the local radio and told them what had happened. The word was out. All the old people of Fairlawns had joined the protest, and they weren't going to give up, not ever. Overhead patio heaters arrived from Mantova, the Italian restaurant in Fore Street. More blankets and duvets and pillows were brought in from the families all around than they knew what to do with. An ambulance came and parked nearby, on permanent stand-by. The television cameras arrived again, but national television this

 207

time, and soon a whole posse of reporters. Paddywack became the centre of attention. It was Miss Carter who told them that Paddywack was their mascot. "He's not leaving and we're not leaving," she declared, not till the Council change their minds."

The police were there too, and in numbers, as a huge crowd began to gather. And all the while the old people sat there, wrapped in their blankets alongside Joe, and Paddywack would walk from one to the other, stopping by each of them for a few minutes, to rest his head on their laps – and to be given a biscuit. By now the cars weren't just hooting, and the lorries weren't just honking. Some of them were actually stopping, and the drivers would get out and come up on to the grass verge to shake hands. More police arrived because of the traffic congestion, and because the crowds all along the pavements were spilling out on to the road.

A police inspector came up to speak to the old people and tried to persuade them to end their protest. He said they were causing a public

nuisance, that he'd have to take action if they didn't move. "What are you going to do?" Miss Carter asked him. "Are you going to arrest us?

Are you going to arrest Paddywack too?" And when they started up their singing again, he had to retreat. It was a song they all knew, an old favourite.

Miss Carter had suggested they should sing it, because of Paddywack of course, but also because everyone at Fairlawns knew it had been Marion's favourite song:

> *This old man, he played one,*
> *He played knick knack on my drum,*
> *With a knick knack paddywack,*
> *Give a dog a bone,*
> *This old man came rolling home!*

They sang it and they sang it, over and over. And then the whole crowd was joining in, belting it out up and down the road.

Soon dozens of relatives had turned up, to support the protest. A few of them did try to persuade the old people to go back indoors, but none of them would. They stayed right where they were, and many of their relatives and friends were so inspired that they stayed on with them, in solidarity. As the streetlights came on and the evening darkened, everyone began to feel the first nip of frost in the air. Mrs Bellamy made a statement to all the gathered reporters. "We're all going inside now," she said, "because it's getting too cold. But we'll be out again in the morning, you can be sure of that." And as they left, the crowd clapped and cheered them all the way up the drive.

In the warmth of the house, those that could stay awake watched themselves on the television news that evening, and that's when they discovered just what an impact their protest had had, and also what was still going on under the glare of the floodlights right outside their front door. The world's press was there now, and hundreds of local people were still gathered on the grass verge. It was Lynn, the paramedic from the hospital, that they happened to be interviewing.

"What you maybe don't know," she was saying, "is that Joe Mahoney's wife, Marion, was looked after in Fairlawns for nearly five years, until she died a couple of months ago. He knows better than anyone how good this place is, and what a crime it would be to close it down. So do I, so does everyone here. And don't think he'll give up, because he won't, nor will any of them." She was looking straight into the camera. "And if you're watching up there in Fairlawns, good on you! Good on you, Joe! Good on you, Paddywack! We're all with you, the whole town." And another great cheer went up. And then they weren't cheering any more, they were singing. It was *Knick Knack Paddywack*, and they were singing it out so loud that the reporter had to shout to make himself heard.

"We asked the Council if they had anything to say, but they refused to make anyone available this evening for comment."

Heartening as all this was Joe found it difficult that night to keep his spirits up. He knew that the old people couldn't sustain their protest for very long, that there was a limit to their endurance. Many of them were very frail. All night long he lay awake, agonising about it. He decided to give it one last day, and then call it off if the Council hadn't changed their mind by the evening.

The next morning, after breakfast, as Joe and Paddywack led the old people down the drive, Joe saw there were hundreds of supporters waiting for them, gathered on the grass verge and all along the pavement below. Some of them were holding up a new banner that read. "Paddywack for Prime Minister!" There was more clapping and whistling and whooping, and then everyone started singing

Knick Knack Paddywack all over again – it really had become the anthem of the protest. It was all a bit much for Paddywack, whose ears were twitching constantly with anxiety. He thrust his head in under Joe's hand for reassurance. The reassurance was mutual. As the song rang out, as he felt Paddywack there right beside him, Joe began to be hopeful once again. But an hour later, with all the exultation and excitement over, with the cold gnawing at him, hope gave way to despair. He glanced across at all the old people, heard their wheezing and their coughing, and saw the suffering in their faces. He knew then he had to bring this to an end, and soon, that some of them might not last out the day.

The crowd was still there in vast numbers all that morning, and so was the press. There were vans with satellite dishes all down the road now. Everyone was watching and waiting. Joe was just brewing up again when he looked up and he saw the policeman – it was the same inspector as the day before – come striding across the grass verge towards him. He had a piece of paper in his hand.

"What's that?" Joe asked. "A warrant for my arrest?"

The police inspector shook his head. "You'd better read it," he said, handing it to Joe. It was a press release.

"Fairlawns Nursing Home. After due and careful consideration, and in the light of the strength of local feeling on this issue, the Council has decided to cancel plans for the closure of Fairlawns."

Joe read it twice, just to be sure there was no mistake, that it really was true. Then he read it aloud, loud enough for everyone to hear.

The cheer that went up was mighty. Total strangers hugged one another. Mrs Bellamy, who was not generally a hugging sort of person, went up and hugged the police inspector, because no one else had.

"What was that for?" he asked.

"Because it's a great moment," she told him,
"and because you brought the good news. Mind
you, if you'd brought bad news, I'd have wrung
your neck."

Cynical old reporters shook their heads and wiped their eyes. Joe himself was so relieved and so happy as he went to thank all the old people one by one, but he could tell that Paddywack just wanted to get away and have some peace and quiet. He could feel him hiding behind his legs, nudging him, and pushing his head into his hand.

He bent down to stroke him. "You hate all this noise, don't you?" he said. "But at least it's a happy noise. Don't you worry, all this fuss and bother will soon be over, and then we can go back to the barge. It'll be just the two of us then, all right?"

But the fuss and bother was not over as soon as Joe might have hoped. Back in Fairlawns there were doctors and nurses everywhere, examining every one of the old people to make sure that none of them was suffering any serious after-effects from the whole experience. One or two were finding it difficult to get warm again and were taken off to hospital with suspected hypothermia. When everything had settled down a bit, Mrs Bellamy and Miss Carter insisted – and they would listen to no argument about it – that Joe should stay on in Fairlawns for a few days, at least until he was strong enough to leave. "And we will decide when that will be," said Miss Carter very firmly.

In fact Joe didn't mind one bit, and in the end, neither did Paddywack. There could never have been a more adored dog in all the world. He revelled in all the loving attention, luxuriated in the warmth of the fire and was offered biscuits almost constantly. Joe and Paddywack were the heroes of the hour, and both were spoiled rotten by everyone at Fairlawns. It was nearly a week before Mrs Bellamy and Miss Carter declared that Joe was fit enough to be allowed to go home.

On the last night there was a celebration supper, to mark the occasion. Everyone got dressed-up for it. Miss Carter wore pink, as she always did for special occasions. Joe brushed Paddywack until he shone, and Mrs Bellamy tied a spotted handkerchief around his neck. They had candles and wine and music. Miss Carter made a speech thanking Joe and Paddywack for saving Fairlawns. The whole evening was like a long goodbye, and when it was over Joe wanted no more fond farewells. So they left early the next morning while it was still dark, while everyone was still asleep. He crept out of Fairlawns with Paddywack and drove home to the barge.

Joe talked all the way there. "Just you and me now, old son," he said, "and *The Lady Marion*." He

 221

looked across at Paddywack, who seemed a bit down. "You miss those old people back at Fairlawns, don't you? Loved you to bits, didn't they?" It was a few moments before he spoke again. "I want you to know something, Paddywack. I may not *ooh* and *aah* over you like they did, but it doesn't mean I don't love you just as much. And with me it's not because you're beautiful, not because of your big brown eyes. It's because you stuck by me. That's what best mates are for, right? My best mate, that's what you were, and that's what you are. That's what we're always going to be, you and me, best mates."

Suddenly Paddywack perked up, ears pricked and happy as if he'd understood every word.

"Time to move on Paddywack. This whole town is full of memories, good memories mostly, but without Marion they'll be sad memories and I reckon they'll only get sadder. I need new places, new faces. Never go back, never go back. I don't know if it's the same for dogs, but I don't think people were made to stay put at all. I mean, look at us, look at all those houses – little boxes every one of them. Most of us live in little boxes like that all our lives. That's what I've done anyway. We don't really want to. It's like we build our own prisons. All right, we may go on holiday from time to time, so we can pretend we're free for a while, but we always come back to our same little box. I don't think that's natural. What about you, Paddywack? Are you the wandering kind? I hope so, I really hope so. Just so long as you don't wander away from me."

It took no more than a few days for Joe to install the potato oven in *The Lady Marion*. He tried to sell the Tattyvan all over town, but being the odd shape it was that didn't prove at all easy. In the end he had to give it away as scrap. "That van was good to me, Paddywack," he said. "Still, it was scrap when I got it, and now it'll be scrap again. That's recycling, nothing to get fussed about I suppose. But all the same it makes me sad."

Paddywack wasn't listening. He was racing off down the towpath towards the barge, scattering ducks and moorhens as he went. He never bothered with the gangplank. He just leaped across on to the deck and made his way at once to the bow, already his favourite place on *The Lady Marion*, where he stood stock still, on the lookout for anything that moved, swans

swimming by or dogs on the towpath, or a flurry of ducks flying over.

That same afternoon Joe started the engine and cast off. The barge moved slowly away from the bank and down the canal, Paddywack still on lookout and Joe at the wheel. Day after day, if the weather was fine, that's where Paddywack would be, up on the bow, like a ship's figurehead, searching always for new excitements and new adventures. He loved to watch the world drift by,

because the world was always changing around him, there was always something new to see or smell or hope for. Sometimes, if the barge came close enough to the bank and Paddywack felt like a run, he'd leap off on to the towpath and go for a sprint. Any unfortunate rabbit or rat caught out in the open, any cat out hunting, was soon sent scurrying away. And with a bit of luck there could even be another dog to play with or race against. Joe loved watching him as he ran circles round every dog he met.

When they came to locks, Paddywack had a routine – Joe thought it was because he didn't like being left behind on the barge. Paddywack would jump out and go and sit up by the lock gates. From there he would oversee Joe at work, as he opened and shut the gates, manoeuvring *The Lady Marion* in and out. Then, as Joe throttled up again Paddywack would spring back on board, and at once resume his lookout post on the bow.

In the evenings they'd tie up somewhere, mostly in a town or a village if they could, and he would sit there beside Joe as he served his customers their baked potatoes, but he was still on lookout. Any cheesy potato skins dropped on the towpath were very quickly discovered and snaffled up. And when the weather was too miserable to travel, then they'd hunker down in the warmth of the cabin and while away the hours with sleep or bacon butties – and knitting, Joe's new hobby. Paddywack was fascinated with Joe's knitting. He couldn't seem to take his eyes off the clicking needles. "Marion taught me years ago," Joe told him one evening. "She said it was good for mind-eye coordination, keeps your brain alive, she said. But I never really took to it. But then, after she died, I found her needles one day and her wool. So I thought I'd take it up again, and make more bobble hats like mine. We'll sell them, like the tatties. Every little helps."

For a year or more, Joe and Paddywack drifted through the seasons in peace and contentment. Hardly a boat passed them by on the canal without some flattering comment about Paddywack, about how beautiful he looked standing there on the bow, or how graceful and powerful he was as he streaked along the towpath. Joe could have wished for a few compliments about his beloved barge, that he had so painstakingly and meticulously restored. But barge owners, as he was discovering, were rather too proud of their own boats to have much enthusiasm for anyone else's.

For Joe there were still moments, usually late in the evening, when memories of Marion would come flooding back and his grief took hold of him again. But Paddywack would always be there beside him through these difficult times. He seemed to sense Joe's need for comfort and company and would settle close to his chair, or rest his head on Joe's knee. "I bless the day I found you," Joe told him one night as Paddywack climbed up on to his bunk beside him. "Or did you find me? I don't suppose we'll ever know, will we, old son?"

It happened on an afternoon much like any other. *The Lady Marion* was cruising along the canal into a town, with Paddywack at the bow as usual. Joe called out to him from the wheel. "We'll go under that bridge and the next one, and that'll bring us just about into the centre of town, I reckon. Not far Paddywack. We could do good tatty business here. Might even sell a bobble hat or two." As they passed under the first bridge Paddywack started barking, the echo of it loud all around them. Joe knew there was nothing unusual about this. Paddywack loved barking as they went under bridges, but this time he didn't stop when they came out into the sunlight again, and Joe thought that was odd. There was the sound of children playing nearby. Joe looked back over his shoulder and saw a school playground by the bridge, full of raucous children running around. By now Paddywack wasn't just barking, he was yelping and tearing up and down the deck, frantic to get off.

There was a strange smell in the air, Joe noticed, sweet and sour like the brown sauce he loved on his bacon butties, and Joe wondered where it was coming from. Ahead of them, about 400 metres away was the next bridge. There was a pair of swans swimming side by side towards it, with half a dozen cygnets bobbing along behind them. Joe thought then it might be the swans Paddywack was getting so worked up about. Or maybe it was the sound of the children in the playground that was exciting him. He noticed Paddywack stopping from time to time to lift his nose and scent the air. But then he'd be racing up and down the deck again, barking wildly, his tail whirling. Joe had never seen him so agitated. He called out to him, trying to calm him down, but Paddywack wasn't listening.

Joe could see what Paddywack was going to do. There was nothing whatever he could do about it. There was no time. All he could do was watch as Paddywack took a running jump and landed in the canal.

By the time Joe had managed to slow the barge down, Paddywack was already clambering out of the water and haring off down the towpath. Joe shouted after him, but he knew it was pointless, that Paddywack was too far away by now to hear him. He could only look on in horror as Paddywack bounded up the steps by the bridge, and then ran straight out into the road. A huge lorry was coming over the bridge. Joe heard the blast of a horn and the screeching of tyres.

"Paddywack!" he cried. "Oh my God, Paddywack!"

It was cold in the water, but I hardly noticed it. I was scrambling out and running, running where my legs took me, knowing Patrick would be waiting for me. I was up the steps then and dashing across the road. I didn't care about the cars all around me, or the lorry bearing down on me. I knew the way home and nothing would stop me getting there. I was going home. I was going back to Patrick. I raced along the pavement, dodging and weaving as I went. Everything around me was so familiar, the trees, the lamp posts, the houses, then I was in the street where I once lived, where Patrick lived.

The gate was open when I got there, but I hurdled the garden wall anyway as I always used to do. I was leaping up and down outside the front door, scrabbling and scratching at it, and barking, barking, barking. But Patrick didn't come. No one came. I decided I'd wait. He'd be bound to come back soon. So I sat down by the door and listened for Patrick's voice, listened for his footsteps. But all the voices I heard were strangers' voices and all the footsteps, strangers' footsteps. There were one or two who stopped to stare at me for a while. One of them was a boy with a little terrier on a lead who was trying to pull away from him, straining to come through the front gate and meet me. I knew that terrier at once – we'd chased each other around up in the park in the old days, I was sure of it. So I went after him.

When they crossed the road I crossed with them. The boy tried to shoo me away, but I ignored him. And all the while the terrier was looking back at me, often having to be dragged along. Only when they started up the hill did I recognise exactly where I was. Only then did I know for sure where they were going, and where I was going too. I didn't need them as pathfinders any more. I knew my own way. I raced past them, through the wide gates at the top of the road, and out into the park, the place Patrick always took me to play. The place I loved best in the whole world. I knew every path, every waste bin, every bench. There were children everywhere, dogs everywhere, and there at the top of the hill ahead of me was the bench I remembered, our bench, Patrick's bench, my bench. There was someone up there, but I was still too far away to see who it was. I galloped up that hill, faster, faster with every stride.

Only now I wasn't alone. I had another dog with me, running along beside me, silver-grey and shining.

And he was fast, as fast as I was. Neck and neck we raced one another up towards the bench. And there was Patrick waiting for me, just as he always had been.

"You've found a friend then?" he said. Patrick was bigger than I remembered him, broader, taller, and his voice had changed. But it was Patrick all right. I leaned myself up against him, and felt his hand on my head, smoothing my ears gently. "A friendly friend too," he went on. "I had a greyhound a bit like you once. You're fawn though. He was gold, gold as the sun. He wasn't as big as you are, and you're a bit white round the muzzle too. And he was fast, really fast, a lot faster than you." He turned his attention to the silver-grey dog who'd jumped up and was on two legs now, his paws on Patrick's chest. "He was faster than you too, you big softie," he said, shrugging him off. "Go on, now you've found someone your own size, go and play with him. Off you go. Go on boy! Go, go, go!"

They were the words I was waiting for. Off I went, off we went together, the silver-grey dog and me, racing round and round the top of the hill. I was loving it and hating it all at the same time. Patrick didn't recognise me as I recognised him. But I was not forgotten, he had remembered me. I ran up to him and bounded about him, barking at him, trying to make him know me. But it was the other dog he knew, the other dog he loved, not me.

He threw sticks for us, and time and again I dropped them at his feet and sat down to wait for him to throw them again, just as I'd always done. Still he did not know me.

I was racing after yet another stick when I saw Joe come puffing up the path towards us. He was so tired out he could hardly speak. All he could say was, "Paddywack, Paddywack!"

"Is he yours?" Patrick asked him. "Run off, did he?"

Joe nodded, still quite unable to speak. "He's been here for half and hour or so," Patrick went on. "I once had a greyhound like him, must be over five years ago now. He ran off too."

By now Joe had recovered a little. "He's never run off before, I don't understand it. It's not like him at all. I've been looking all over. Someone down by the pond said I should come and have a look in the park. There's always dogs up there, dozens of dogs, and dogs like other dogs. He was right, wasn't he? Thank goodness."

For a moment Joe and Patrick said nothing more. They looked at us lying there at their feet, panting our hearts out. "Where did you get yours?" Patrick asked.

"I guess we just found each other," Joe replied. "Strange meeting really, when I think back on it. Just the luckiest thing. Right time, right dog, right place. What about you?"

"Same with me, I suppose," said Patrick. "When my

first dog ran off – Best Mate he was called – I looked everywhere for him. It happened here too, right here in the park. I came back every day for months. I was sure he'd come back. But he never did. He just disappeared. So in the end my dad and me, we went down to the rescue centre. I wanted another greyhound. I like greyhounds. They're the best. I love to watch them run. They run like cheetah-dogs. In fact they're the third fastest animal on earth, after a cheetah and a prong-horned antelope – did you know that? I could watch them and watch them. And they're kind too. I like that." Patrick glanced at his watch. "Homework. I'd better be going, I suppose. See you," he said, and he ran off, the silver-grey dog trotting at his heels.

I watched until they disappeared over the hill, under the trees. I found I wasn't so sad any more. I was just glad I'd seen him.

"Let's go home, Paddywack," said Joe. "Bacon butties for tea, and biscuits for afters. All right?"

As we walked away I looked back over my shoulder, hoping to catch a last glimpse of Patrick, but he was gone.

I miss him, like I miss Alfie, like I miss Becky. But I've got Joe now, and Joe's got me, and we're fine.

MORE THAN A STORY

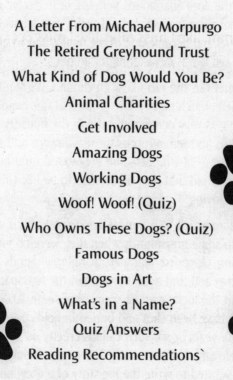

Dear Reader,

Some ten years ago we went to a rescue centre looking for a dog and came away with a lurcher puppy. We called her Bercelet. I remember looking into the cages and wondering where all these dogs had come from, whose lives they had been part of. All sorts of questions came at once into my head. Had the owner died? Were the dogs abandoned perhaps, or neglected or abused? What were the lives behind their eyes? Anyway Bercelet stayed with us and became one of the family, and when she died three years ago it was devastating for all of us.

When Bercelet ran she ran like a greyhound. We simply loved standing there watching her. She seemed at her happiest at full stretch. She was very gentle and calm in the house, very attached to us and reliant on us for reassurance and affection. The more I heard of whippets and greyhounds and lurchers, the more I realised that they all seemed to be like this, very trusting and loving.

Then I read an article in a Sunday newspaper about what had happened to some greyhounds when they were no longer any use for racing. Of course many ex-racing greyhounds end up in rescue centres and find good homes, but the newspaper article wasn't about the lucky ones. It seems that some 10,000 greyhounds have been shot and buried in fields over a period of about fifty years or so. Such callous cruelty on such a massive scale angered me greatly. The more I thought about it the more I wanted to write the life story of a greyhound. And this is what I've done.

Michael Morpurgo

retired greyhound trust

What happens to greyhounds when they reach the end of their racing career?

The Retired Greyhound Trust, or RGT, is a national charity dedicated to finding good homes for greyhounds when they can no longer race.

Set up in 1975, and with seventy branches throughout the United Kingdom, the Retired Greyhound Trust has found homes for nearly 40,000 greyhounds. A new home could be an approved kennel, or a family home, and the RGT actively seeks people willing to care for a greyhound, and makes sure that a potential new owner is suitable. As well as ensuring that the re-homed greyhounds are healthy, the RGT has close links with the greyhound racing industry and highlights the importance of providing a good life for retired greyhounds. The charity also raises money to support its work.

The dog on the cover of *Born to Run* has been used by kind courtesy of The Retired Greyhound Trust. Why don't you become a friend of the RGT or join your local RGT branch? If you would like to find out more about the RGT and learn about events the trust may be holding in your area, log on to: **www.retiredgreyhounds.co.uk.**

What Kind of Dog Would You Be?

**We've chosen four types of dogs with very different personalities.
Which one suits you best?**

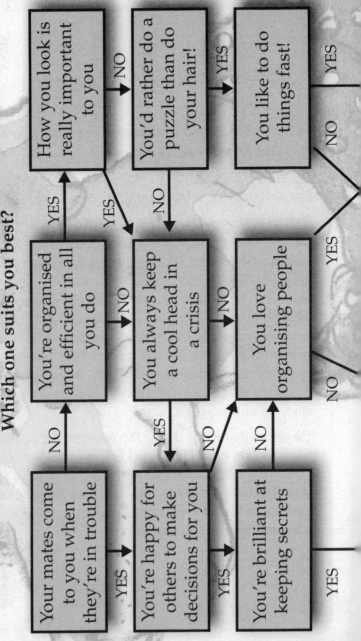

You're worried about putting other people out
— YES → St Bernard
— NO → Poodle

You think of others before yourself
— YES → Poodle
— NO → St Bernard

You are patient and careful
— YES → Sheep Dog
— NO → Greyhound

Winning is more important than taking part
— NO → Sheep Dog
— YES → Greyhound

St Bernard

You're a loyal friend and trusted confidant – a great person to have around in a crisis! But remember to take the time to look after yourself, and don't let others trample all over you!

Poodle

You take pride in your appearance and you really stand out from the crowd. Your confidence and individual style will take you far in life. But be careful – looks aren't everything!

Sheep Dog

You're hard working and intelligent with a talent for difficult tasks. When your friends wants something done, you're on speed-dial! But be careful to let others have their say – remember the power of team work!

Greyhound

You're competitive and athletic – a real high achiever who gets results quickly. But make sure you don't jump the gun – sometimes slow and steady wins the race!

Animal Charities

You may have heard of these animal charities...

Dogs Trust
Set up as the National Canine Defence League (NCDL) in 1891, the Dogs Trust is the largest dog welfare charity in the United Kingdom. Its nationwide network of re-homing centres care for over 11,000 dogs each year. Find out more at: wwwdogstrust.org.uk.

Battersea Dogs and Cats Home
This charity has been rescuing, reuniting, re-housing and rehabilitating animals for over 140 years. For more information and events in your area, check out: www.dogshome.org.

The World Wildlife Fund
Set up in 1961, you may recognise the World Wildlife Fund's panda logo. The largest global charity, the WWF has been instrumental in saving many animals from extinction. Log on to: www.wwf.org to find out more.

RSPCA
The Royal Society for the Prevention of Cruelty to Animals was founded (as the SPCA) in 1824, and the charity campaigns to promote kindness to animals. Look up: www.rspca.org.uk for more information.

...but have you heard of these?

Dog Rescue – Ireland
This is a voluntary Irish animal charity dedicated to rescuing and re-homing Irish Greyhounds (ex-racing and domestic) that would otherwise be destroyed: www.dogrescueireland.com.

The Donkey Sanctuary, Sidmouth, Devon
Since 1969 this charity has housed over 12,000 donkeys, and now has over forty-five welfare officers who act on reports of cruelty or neglect of donkeys. For the latest news and information on its open days see: www.thedonkeysanctuary.org.uk.

The Wildlife Hospital Trust (Tiggywinkles), Buckinghamshire
This animal hospital cares for sick and injured hedgehogs, badgers, wild birds, foxes, reptiles and amphibians: www.sttiggywinkles.org.uk.

Wood Green Animal Shelters
Set up on 1924, the Wood Green Animal Shelters rescue and re-home over 6,000 animals a year. For more, check out: www.woodgreen.org.uk.

Why don't you find out what local animal charities there are in your area? Ask in your local library for more information.

Would you like to get involved?

Why don't you...

- Sponsor or adopt an animal •
- Find a charity offering the chance for you to 'own' a virtual pet •
- Make a donation to your favourite animal charity •
- Collect used inkjet cartridges or old mobile phones to help Guide Dogs for the Blind (see website below, and remember to check with the mobile phone owner first!) •
- Offer to volunteer at your local animal rescue centre •
- Give an unwanted animal a home* •

*All pets must be cared for responsibly, and housed in a suitable environment. Check with your local animal charity for advice – if you live in a flat, a large, hairy Wolfhound may not be for you!

Would you like to work with animals?

Why don't you...

- Offer to take a neighbour's dog for a walk •
- Look after a friend's pet while they're on holiday •
- Find out which farms in your area have open days* •
- Are there any stables near you? Try mucking out! •
- Think about a career as a vet or an animal welfare officer – talk to someone at your local veterinary practice or rescue centre for more information – or what about becoming a marine biologist? •

* If you live in an urban area why don't you suggest that your school visits a farm to see how animals are cared for? Go on a farm activity holiday – in the spring you'll see lambs, in the autumn you could help with apple-pressing.

Amazing dogs

Fast dog!
Greyhounds can run up to a speed of about 45 miles per hour, and there are only two faster land mammals: the cheetah, which can reach a speed of 70–75 miles per hour and Thomson's Gazelle, which can reach a speed of 50 miles per hour.

Jumping dog!
The world record for the highest jump by a dog is 68 inches – achieved by a Holly Grey.*

Big dog!
The tallest dog recorded is a Great Dane, which measured 42.2 inches tall.*

Little dog!
A Chihuahua has been officially named as the smallest dog in the world, in terms of length, measuring six inches from the nose to tip of the tail.*

Big ears!
The longest ears on a dog belong to a bloodhound, with a measurement of 13.75 inches (that's longer than the smallest Chihuahua!).*

* Source: the Guinness Book of Records: www.guinnessworldrecords.com

Working dogs

Guide dogs for the blind – www.guidedogs.org.uk
There are 5,000 of these remarkable dogs working in the United Kingdom today. Each animal, predominantly the Labrador, Golden Retriever or German Shepherd breed, is trained to an exceptional standard and gives its owner a degree of mobility they would not have otherwise had.

Hearing dogs for the deaf – www.hearingdogs.org.uk
Hearing dogs change the lives for their owners, alerting them to sounds non-deaf people take for granted. The dogs give their owners a sense of security and have saved lives by alerting their owners to dangers in the home.

Water rescue dogs
The Newfoundland breed is especially built for swimming, and their life-saving ability in the water means they're perfect as water rescue dogs – not only for locating and rescuing people, but boats too.

Police dogs
The police use tracking dogs such as Labradors to find missing objects or persons, guard dogs such as Doberman Pinchers to help detain criminals and Spaniels or Collie dogs to sniff out illegal drugs or explosives.

Awards
Did you know there was an animal bravery award? The PDSA Dickin Medal, founded in 1943, acknowledges outstanding acts of bravery by animals serving in the Armed Forces. The Animal awards programme exists to recognise animal bravery and devotion to duty.

Woof! Woof!

Listen to a dog barking – is it a Woof, an Arf, a Bow Wow, a Ruff or a Yip Yip? Or perhaps it's a Ouah Ouah?

Different languages have different words for a dog's bark – and sometimes more than one! Can you guess which countries these dogs come from?

1. Voff Voff
2. Wang Wang
3. Bau Bau
4. Ouah Ouah
5. Woef Woef
6. Vov Vov
7. Wau Wau
8. Hav Hav

Answers on page 255

Who owns these dogs?

Each of these famous dogs has an equally famous owner, but who are they?

1. Snowy
2. Gnasher
3. K9
4. Gromit
5. Dogmatix
6. Cabal
7. Argos
8. Scooby Doo

WOOF

Answers on page 255

Famous dogs

Space dog
The first dog to orbit the Earth was called Laika. She flew
aboard the Russian satellite Sputnik 2 in 1957.

Logo dog
If you shop in HMV, look at the logo. Did you
know that HMV stands for His Master's Voice?
The dog, called Nipper, is listening to the voice
of his master playing on a gramophone.

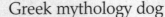

Greek mythology dog
Cerebus – the hound of Hades – was said to have
three heads, a serpent tail and the heads of snakes
on his back. Not one to meet on a dark night...

Royal dog
A corgi named Dookie started the Queen's love of
the breed, but the royal family has also owned
Pomeranians, Labradors and Japanese Chin dogs.

Faithful dog
In 1858, a man named John Gray was buried in old Greyfriars
Churchyard, Edinburgh. For fourteen long years the dead man's
faithful dog, a Skye Terrier, kept watch over the
grave. A statue of the dog, Greyfriars' Bobby,
can be seen on the spot where he kept
watch.

Dogs in art

The earliest European images of dogs are over 12,000 years old and can be found in cave paintings in Spain. Images of dogs are depicted in Egyptian wall paintings and hieroglyphics and you can also see images of dogs in classical Greek pottery and sculpture.

The following artists have all featured dogs in their work: George Stubbs, Sir Edwin Landseer, John Constable and David Hockney. Have you seen any of their work? If you are interested in paintings of greyhounds why don't you look at the work of Albrect Durer? Visit a local or national museum and see how many images of dogs you can find.

Don't forget to look for paintings depicting St Hubert, the patron saint of dogs.

If you get a chance to visit the Guggenheim Museum, Bilbao, Spain, you will see a gigantic sculpture called 'Puppy' made of stainless steel and flowering plants.

Get creative

Try this...

- Draw a picture of your favourite animal

- Make an animal mask

- Write a story about an animal – or why not be inspired by Michael Morpurgo and write from the point of view of the animal?

- Get some chicken wire, old newspaper and wallpaper paste. Shape the chicken wire into an animal; tear up the newspaper and dip it in the wallpaper paste; lay it over the chicken wire to make your own 3-D sculpture (it doesn't have to be life-size – particularly if you like elephants...)

What's in a name?

The canine hero of *Born to Run* is given a different name by each of his owners. For Patrick, he's Best Mate; for Becky, he's Brighteyes; and finally, for the Tattyman, he's Paddywack. Here are some of the most popular names for dogs – would you have chosen one of these?

Max	Duke	Maggie	Sandy
Jake	Cody	Molly	Sasha
Buddy	Casey	Lady	Abby
Bailey	Buster	Sadie	Ginger
Sam	Rocky	Lucy	Daisy

Quiz Answers

Woof! Woof!
Did you guess the right country?

1. Iceland
2. China
3. Italy
4. France

5. Holland
6. Sweden
7. Germany
8. Russia

Who owns these dogs?
Did you guess these famous owners?

1. Tintin
2. Dennis the Menace
3. Dr Who
4. Wallace

5. Obelix
6. King Arthur
7. Odysseus
8. Shaggy

Reading Recommendations

If you enjoy books about animals why don't you read the following books by Michael Morpurgo?

The Amazing Story of Adolphus Tips

It's 1943, and Lily Tregenze lives on a farm in the village of Slapton – a place the war hasn't reached – until she and the other villagers are told to move out of their homes. While the Allied forces practise their landings for D-Day on Lily's beach, there's one villager who hasn't left – Lily's cat Adolphus Tips... A heart-warming tale of love and courage.

Toro! Toro!

Antonito lives on a farm with his family in Spain. When he helps deliver a bull, Antonito names him Paco and the two become inseparable. But then Antonito learns that his uncle is a bullfighter, and that Paco is to be sent to the bullring. Antonito knows he must act, but then the Spanish Civil War changes everything...

Dear Olly

The story of Matt and Olly is lyrically entwined with the story of a bird called Hero. When Matt decides to work in Africa, his sister Olly is charged with protecting a nest of young birds in their garden. But only one young bird survives and Olly names it Hero. Hero's flight from England to Africa links Olly and Matt in this poignant story of family love.

The Butterfly Lion

When young Bertie is sent away from his parents' farm in Africa to attend school in England, he is heartbroken to leave his pet white lion cub. Bertie vows that the two will meet again, whatever it takes in this moving tale about a lifelong friendship.

The Dancing Bear

High in a mountain village, an abandoned bear cub is adopted by a lonely child. The girl and bear become firm friends – they are loved by the other villagers and safe from the outside world. Safe until a film crew arrives in search of a dancing bear...

Recommended books by michael morpurgo